"Shawn!" Jackie yelled. "Don't give up!"

He blinked, as if coming out of a nightmare. Pain like he'd never experienced rushed through all his muscles. He fought to focus. Jackie lay flat on her stomach on the lake's treacherous ice. She could plunge through right next to Shawn at any second.

"Put both hands on my pack and don't let go," she ordered. She twisted slightly away from him. The momentum pulled Shawn up enough to get his elbows on top of the ice. Jackie's back arched, and she stabbed the ice with a stick end to anchor them. "Try to climb!"

He reached six inches past his first grasp. Jackie pulled on the stick and slid farther away. The strain it had to be causing her gave Shawn newfound strength. He would not let her die for him. Coming out of a frozen lake, threatening to pull him back in, proved to be the hardest pull-up he'd ever endured. His chest hit the ice.

Crack...

Heather Woodhaven earned her pilot's license, rode a hot-air balloon over the safari lands of Kenya, parasailed over Caribbean seas, lived through an accidental detour onto a black-diamond ski trail in Aspen, and snorkeled among stingrays before becoming a mother of three and wife of one. She channels her love for adventure into writing characters who find themselves in extraordinary circumstances.

Books by Heather Woodhaven

Love Inspired Suspense

Calculated Risk
Surviving the Storm
Code of Silence
Countdown
Texas Takedown
Tracking Secrets
Credible Threat
Protected Secrets
Wilderness Sabotage

Twins Separated at Birth

Undercover Twin
Covert Christmas Twin

True Blue K-9 Unit: Brooklyn

Chasing Secrets

Visit the Author Profile page at Harlequin.com.

WILDERNESS SABOTAGE

HEATHER WOODHAVEN

LOVE INSPIRED SUSPENSE
INSPIRATIONAL ROMANCE

LOVE INSPIRED® SUSPENSE
INSPIRATIONAL ROMANCE

ISBN-13: 978-1-335-40311-7

Wilderness Sabotage

Copyright © 2020 by Heather Humrichouse

Recycling programs for this product may not exist in your area.

This edition published by arrangement with Harlequin Books S.A.

For questions and comments about the quality of this book, please contact us at CustomerService@Harlequin.com.

Love Inspired
22 Adelaide St. West, 40th Floor
Toronto, Ontario M5H 4E3, Canada
www.Harlequin.com

Printed in U.S.A.

As the Father hath loved me,
so have I loved you: continue ye in my love.
–*John* 15:9

To my husband: Thank you for being
my research partner and first reader. Your reactions
make writing all the more enjoyable. Love you.

ONE

Jackie Dutton flipped up the back collar of her navy peacoat to brace against the bitter wind. Her boots crunched over the thick snow, hours away from Boise—hours away from *any* city—in the middle of the mountainous desert terrain of southern Idaho. She would do almost anything to get a story. Unfortunately, her editor used the knowledge to his advantage.

She walked alongside Hank Swain, an older foreman whose face displayed the evidence of many years spent squinting into the sun. He led her around green and red shipping containers that unintentionally looked like Christmas decorations for the mountains. "We're talking about a two-hundred-acre project," Hank said, stopping next to a snowmobile. "So it's hard to give you a proper tour, but I think I've shown you the basics. We finished building that control structure, but as you can see, we've only started on the air-cooling assembly."

She glanced up at what looked like fans the size of airplane engines on top of fifty-foot-high poles with metallic ladders at every corner. "These acts of sabotage must be extremely upsetting for you and your crew," Jackie said.

"That's an understatement." The foreman gestured with his hand at the damaged crane. "We specialize in building at remote sites no matter the season. It's why we win most of our bids from government contracts, but winter weather makes the challenges harder."

"Isn't this a private contract?"

"No." He shook his head. "We're on federal land. Everything the McDowell Geothermal Company does is by permit and lease. Even the bid for construction had to be approved by the Bureau of Land Management."

From her rudimentary understanding, the geothermal plant was designed to drill down to the hot water underneath the ground and use the steam to produce electricity, making it a valuable renewable energy source—assuming the sabotage stopped long enough for them to finish building.

Swain spun around and pointed north. "We finished the access road you drove up on before the first snow, at least, but we can't afford to let sabotage slow us down."

The sun hovered low against the horizon of the surrounding foothills. Days ended even earlier up in the mountains, which meant she'd be driving in the dark if she didn't wrap up the interview fast. "So far, your equipment and tools have been targeted. Any ideas on who wants to sabotage your efforts here?"

He shrugged. "Off the record?"

How was she ever supposed to get a promotion-worthy story if everything was off the record? Jackie forced a pleasant smile.

He folded his arms against his chest. "Environmental groups get riled up every time anything is constructed. Some bird nest gets disturbed…"

No news there. The CEO and plant manager had given her the same answer on the phone. The foreman rounded the corner of the control building and led her back to her car. Except, she couldn't go yet. She had no story.

"Would any of your crew be willing to talk to me?"

He shook his head. "Even if they were, they're on the opposite edge of the site and should have wrapped up for the day." He gestured at his snowmobile, sitting alone. "The closest place my guys can stay is a motel thirty miles away as the crow flies past that line of trees. Would take them a couple hours if they drove it, though they get to go home to their families this weekend. Won't be back until after Christmas." The wind blew an extra hard gust. He glanced at the mountains to the west. "Speaking of which, I better go. They're waiting for me. You should get, too. Radar says storms are coming."

"Well, thank you and merry Christmas." She felt his eyes on her until she got in her car and turned on the ignition. He moved to the snowmobile and took off in the direction of the in-progress drill sites.

She glanced at her phone. One bar of service flickered on and off. She quickly typed a message to her editor.

I think I could find a story here with more time. I'll

need more interviews after the holiday. Don't expect check-in until Monday night.

The bar slid slowly across the screen, but she was unsure it would send until she returned to civilization. It was only Tuesday, but her cousin's wedding festivities started tonight and Friday was Christmas. She was overdue to catch up on family life. Afterward, she would have to return to interview the crew. The real story was never found by talking to supervisors.

Movement entered her peripheral vision. A man with a clipboard strapped to the front of his coat snowmobiled between tall columns she assumed were pipes. In her research, photos of similar geothermal power plants reminded her of a giant circuit board. Instead of capacitors and transistors, there were giant tanks of water and pipes. So if she could remember that her car was at the end of the long red pipe, she'd be able to find her way back safely.

She shoved her phone back in her coat, hustled out of the car and followed the trail of the man with the clipboard. Maybe she could wrap up the story and wouldn't have to come back to this desolate place after all.

"I told you it would bring more attention." A man raised his voice. Jackie couldn't see the speaker, though, as they were past the corner of the control building.

"This is what you pay me for." A second voice, deeper in tone and louder in volume, snapped back. "No one else had any better ideas."

"Well, you went too far. That detect—"

"That's enough. I told you I'd take care of it."

Jackie tensed and strained her ears. Was the first man trying to indicate a detective had been around? She didn't want her presence known quite yet.

"No. You're done," the softer-spoken man said. "Take your stuff and leave."

"I don't think so."

The wind carried a muffled groan and what sounded like a physical struggle.

"Fighting will only make it worse," the deep voice said, eerily calm. "You're dying either way."

The muscles in her stomach tensed at the threat until she could barely breathe. She pulled out her phone. Police would take too long to arrive if the closest city was an hour's drive, but maybe the foreman of the construction crew could turn around on his snowmobile fast enough. No signal. She didn't know if her text message from earlier had even sent.

She peeked around the corner. The man with the clipboard collapsed to the ground, his face devoid of life. The other man pulled something that looked like a syringe out from the man's shoulder—he had injected him right through his coat. He lifted his head.

She pulled back before he could see her. Her left foot missed the sidewalk and sank into the snow with a crunch. Nearby birds stopped singing, and the air grew heavy with silence. Even the wind halted. Had he heard her?

The crunching of his boots on the snow grew louder. The wind picked back up and made it hard to tell if the sound was coming her way, though. Should she bolt for it and risk being seen or hide? She pressed her back up against the building and sidestepped around the corner, taking care to stay on the shoveled sidewalk.

"A little tip," the deep voice announced, though she couldn't see him. "If you're going to hide, next time, don't leave footprints behind."

She glanced down at the cement. Like a wet stamp, the tread of her boots had left their prints on the sidewalk. And the only way back to her car would be to run past him. Of all the times to not have a cell signal.

She couldn't hear his steps anymore. Maybe he was on the sidewalk, too.

She continued to round the building. Her reflection, out of the corner of her eye, gave her pause. She peered into the windows of the building. No light, no sign of life, but the reflection revealed something else. The snowmobile that the man with the clipboard had ridden still had the key hanging from the ignition. She spun around. Her heart beat faster with indecision.

Another crunch of the snow convinced her. She launched off her back heel and ran for it.

"Hey! Come back here!" he yelled. "I just want to talk."

For a split second, she almost slowed down, but the dead body she ran past encouraged her to go faster. She flung her leg over the side of the vehicle and cranked the key. The snowmobile revved to life. Her bare hands covered the handles and twisted.

The vehicle launched forward, jolting her backward slightly, but she clung to the handles and leaned toward them. The man was too close to her car, so she guided the snowmobile around the monstrous construction area and pointed the nose of the vehicle in the direction the construction foreman had traveled. There were tracks in the snow and ice indicating where he'd gone. If she could find him, he would accompany her safely to her car.

A revving engine, twice as loud as hers, growled to life. She dared a look over her shoulder. A four-wheel ATV with giant wheels barreled her way. She focused on the tracks ahead, twisting the throttle of the snowmobile as far as it would go.

The tracks twisted around the construction equipment that bordered the cement pads and drilling equipment that had yet to be installed. They were harder to follow here. She turned into a clearing in between two sections of forest. The man on the ATV would overtake her before she reached the forest, and the foreman wouldn't be able to see her until she rode past the line of trees.

On the left side, next to the drilling pads, a rock wall a hundred feet tall rose up from the ground, a natural fence of the property. The foothills and forest stood in front of her. The murderer continued chase, leaving her only one choice.

She needed to outmaneuver him and get back on the road to her vehicle. His ATV may be fast, but the snowmobile handled sharp curves more gracefully. If she could get to her car with time to spare, surely she could drive away before his ATV overtook her.

She twisted her handle hard to the left. Except, he swung wide and blocked her path. She revved the handles harder and headed for one of the foothills at full throttle. He'd taken away her options, and she'd completely lost sight of where the construction crew tracks had been.

She vaulted up and over the foothill. A thin crevice was ten feet away, running diagonal from southeast to northwest, hidden from her view until now. She gasped, all her breath suddenly gone. She twisted the steering as far as it would go so she wouldn't dive over the cliff. The crevice grew wider into more of a gorge. She rode parallel to it, straining her vision to see if the crevice had an end. Otherwise, how did the crew ever cross?

Ahead, another hundred feet or so, the deep vault disappeared and was replaced by more rolling snowy hills. She'd soon be able to cross over to the forest sections. The ATV quad motor behind her grew louder.

She glanced over her shoulder to gauge how close it was. A solid force punched her in the chest. Her head volleyed backward and forward before her body flew off the snowmobile.

She hit the snow hard and started sliding. Her fingers, stinging from the cold, tried to dig into the snow like grappling hooks. Instead, she slipped downward on an unstoppable path to the edge. Her eyes caught sight of the snow-covered boulder that had crumpled the front nose of the snowmobile.

A whoosh of air swept underneath her coat as gravity took her over the edge into nothingness. A scream tore from her throat. Her hands reached and grabbed blindly. Wood slapped her palms. She wasn't fast enough to grab the branch, though. Another slam of impact hit her, this time right in her stomach.

She couldn't breathe. As she slipped off the branch

or root remains that'd caught her, her fingers gripped the knots. Tears clouded her vision as she swung, holding tightly. *Please let me breathe.* Lightning flashes of pain at her temples stung before she sucked in a huge breath and cried out. Never before had getting the air knocked out of her hurt so much. Still, she clung to the branch, gulping in air. The tips of her boots searched to find a foothold to help carry some of her weight, but she was too far away from the cliff.

The rev of an engine grew closer. Snow clumps tumbled over the cliff's edge. The cold hit the top of her head. She shivered and almost lost her grasp. "Please, God," she whispered. "Not again."

What was the use of trying? She was trapped, and the murderer had just arrived to finish her off.

Shawn Burkett jumped out of his truck. There was no time to lose.

He'd been on his way to check that Pete Wooledge, the field archaeologist, had left before shutting down for the night when he'd spotted a reckless ATV bouncing near the crevice.

Just past the land designated for the geothermal plant was a dangerous area without trails. Only the construction crew had special permission to motor in this direction, but they had strict instructions to follow the approved GPS and stay on the specified route until they reached the safer, groomed trails a few miles away.

Shawn had been ready to chase the driver down to write a ticket before he'd noticed the ATV was following a snowmobile. The moment the driver of the ATV spotted Shawn's approach he'd turned toward the trees, no doubt to hide. Maybe the man had been actually chasing the snowmobile, then.

There was no time to make a report to the field office. Whoever had fallen off the snowmobile had only seconds to spare before that branch gave way and they plummeted hundreds of feet. He grabbed his rescue pack and slapped it on his back. Normally, he took the time to examine the terrain and choose the best anchor before he rappelled off a cliff, but every second counted now. His movements were almost on autopilot, which could get him killed, so he fought to be fast but also mindful.

The rope slipped easily through the hubs of the back wheels on his truck, and within sixty seconds he had the harness, tether and backup extensions set. "Hold on. Bureau of Land Management law enforcement ranger coming to get you." He threw the rope over the edge. "Rope," he called out as a warning.

"I…I'm trying to hold on." A woman's soft voice drifted through the wind.

He pushed down the surge of anger. That driver definitely had been chasing the woman, then. But at the moment, the reasons why weren't important. He checked his carabiner and hitch before testing the rope slack and his grip. "I'll be there in a second. Stay with me. It's hard, but you can do it."

His morning and evening workout routine paid off at times like these. Fitness proved the best defense against such a physically demanding job. He leaned back into nothingness and kicked off. The moment his feet first met air always provided a burst of fear and adrenaline, but growing up in the northwest, he'd spent so many hours rappelling that the motion was almost like second nature. The bottom of his boots reached and gently pushed off the face of the cliff. The sides of the rocky crevice held only the slightest bit of snow in the cracks with only a hint of ice on the parts that got the most shade.

The crack of a branch and a scream from below made his blood run colder than the frigid temperatures. "I'm coming. Hang on!" He slid the rope through his fingers. Too fast and he could lose control, but the woman might not last long enough for a careful descent.

He shoved his soles off the rock face harder than normal and soared down, his gloved fingers loose around the braking rope. His feet dropped right below hers as one of her hands slid off the branch. He gripped the rope tight and let go with his left hand as the branch snapped clean.

His left arm wrapped tightly around her waist and he pitched forward with the sudden weight. The branch narrowly missed them, and he thrust his right foot out to keep their heads from smashing against the rock face.

She gasped and reached for the sharp edges.

"I've got you," he said. "We're going to get out of this together." He shifted his head away from the thick brown hair that was currently in his face. "Grab on to my rope. Stick your legs out and let's balance on the rock. I'll hook us together."

"You sure you got me?" Her voice was steadier, a good sign, and somehow familiar.

"Yes, ma'am. Lean sideways into me, against me." He spoke in soothing tones in hopes she didn't panic or go into shock. "Good. Don't let go of the rope. When you feel safe, I'm going to remove my arm from your waist and fashion an emergency harness."

She turned her head to look at the ropes dangling from his harness and snapped her head up. Their eyes met. "Shawn?" Her voice rose an octave. "What? Why—"

His throat tightened with the same degree of shock in her voice. He studied her features as she stared at him, frozen in the awkward position. The same vibrant blue eyes that never missed a thing, the same mouth that could flash a smile to brighten the darkest of days and the same forehead creased in concentration. The Jackie Dutton he knew felt she had to understand literally everything that crossed her path. Why had someone been chasing her? "I'd like to ask what you're doing here, but—"

She nodded rapidly. "But we should probably focus on getting down safely first. I think it'll be easier if you let me help but continue to make sure I don't fall to my death. May I?" She reached across him and grabbed the section of free rope he had been about to unclip from his harness. She made quick work of wrapping the rope around her chest and looping it over her shoulders with a final knot in the center.

He examined her work, though she'd always been better than him. The daughter of famed reality wilderness star Wolfe Dutton, she'd grown up learning all the techniques her dad demonstrated in his *Surviving with Wolfe* TV series.

Shawn double-checked to make sure her knots were tight enough. "Is rappelling like riding a bike?"

"Hardly. Though when you get trained on knots and rappelling safety from the time you can tie your own shoes, it's hard to forget." She blew out a breath and pointed to the extra carabiner hanging from his tether.

He handed the item over and within a minute she'd adequately latched the rudimentary harness into his system. Snow began falling more heartily from above. An engine—no, multiple engines—revved loudly from above.

"Oh, that's not good…"

"Maybe the driver realized what had happened and recruited help."

"Trust me, Shawn. If it's the driver of that ATV, we don't want his help."

His forehead tightened. He really needed to know how she was forced into this predicament. Jackie would've never been careless enough to snowmobile without knowing the terrain unless it was an emergency. He adjusted his stance. "I'm going to let go of you now. Ready?"

She nodded rapidly, testing the grip, though he noticed she had bare hands and her knuckles were bright red. "Jackie, let me see your palms."

"I can do this."

Jackie had always bristled against help, but her determination could prove deadly if splinters hindered her ability to hold on. "Your palms are probably full of splinters."

Now at his side, she clenched her teeth. "We don't have time to argue."

More chunks of snow fell from above. Her eyes flicked upward. "Shawn, please tell me you didn't use your truck as an anchor."

"Do you have any idea how much that truck weighs? And there are chains on the tires. It's perfectly safe." He whipped his head around to follow her gaze. Hard chunks of frozen snow careened over the edge, barely missing their location. His truck slid forward. How? He'd put the parking brake on, he was sure of it.

"I knew it." Her voice shook. "They're coming to finish the job. Is there enough rope to get us all the way down?"

"Without making a new anchor?" The rope was four hundred feet long, but this particular spot in the crevice might be more than five hundred feet deep. The truck moved again, this time faster, as if being pushed to the edge. He didn't understand what was happening except for what would be the result.

His gaze searched the rock face wildly. Twenty feet to the left, he found what looked like their only chance. He pointed. "There. Can you get to that ledge?"

Her eyes widened in horror but she nodded. Shawn looked over his shoulder once more and understood her raw fear. The side of his truck hung precariously over the edge. "Now!"

He twisted and pressed off the rock face with his right foot. He reared back as far as possible. The momentum swung him forward like a pendulum. He grabbed the back of Jackie's coat with his left hand, pulling her farther out from the cliffs in case he misjudged the trajectory, to prevent her from slamming against the sharp rock wall.

She reached forward to the ledge with her arm and right leg outstretched. The moment her feet touched it, he also extended his feet, but more to serve as brakes. The soles of his boots hit against the ledge and stopped his trajectory. Except, a pendulum always swings backward. Jackie spun around as he fought against the pull. She grabbed the front of his harness and dropped her weight in a squat so he wouldn't pull them both off.

The way she tugged at his jacket forced his satellite phone up and out of its holder. The phone soared down just as he found his equilibrium. He never heard it hit the ground.

They both panted, clinging to each other on the small outcropping. "We made it," she whispered. The echo in between the two rock walls amplified her words. But that wasn't the only sound the echo magnified. The creaking of his truck reverberated once more as it was completely pushed over the edge.

"The rope!" Jackie searched him over. "Shawn! The knots!"

Every muscle in his body tensed. He'd knotted both ends of the rope for safety so even if he let go or fell, the knots in the ropes would save him. Those same knots would make sure they were dragged down with the truck. They would be snapped right down to the bottom and slammed into his favorite hunk of metal.

"Unhook yourself from me." If he was going down, he wasn't taking her with him.

"Don't be ridiculous." Their hands fumbled, both searching for the same thing on the rope. The ATC device prevented the rope from twisting or tangling when someone rappelled but also kept their harnesses attached to the rope. They had to get it detached. His thumb reached the carabiner and spun the lock with more force than he'd ever used.

Her hands grabbed the clip before he could and she squeezed. The device released and shot away from them like a rocket, carrying the rope down to the ground without them.

The truck spun in the air and hit the bottom of the canyon floor with a sickening crunch. As if to ensure Shawn understood the severity of his truck's demise, it continued to creak and groan. It could have been them, broken and mangled at the bottom, if they hadn't unhooked in time. "My truck," he said. "We've been through a lot together."

"Well, it looks like *we're* about to be through a lot together. Namely, how are we going to get down from here without getting killed?"

His gut twisted at her words. He was trapped on the side of a cliff with the woman he'd once loved and, judging by the way she looked at him, she still hated him.

TWO

The last time Jackie had been trapped in the wilderness was as a headstrong sixteen-year-old, ready to prove to her father that she was just as capable as her fraternal twin, Eddie. So she'd set out on her dad's trademarked wilderness survival test without telling anyone.

Everything was fine until she'd come across a mountain lion that scared her, ironically, right off the edge of another cliff. She'd found an outcropping, complete with a cave, and tried not to spook the nesting bats as she'd waited, with a broken arm and twisted ankle, for twenty-two painful and terrifying hours until search and rescue found her. Waiting to be rescued while injured had been the last straw.

Never again, she'd told her parents. Never again would she go camping or backpacking or hiking. It didn't matter that the test had been her idea. She wouldn't so much as participate in a campfire in the backyard with s'mores.

She'd experienced her fill of survival training her entire childhood, and it took waiting with a broken bone to realize she never wanted anything to do with experiencing the wild again, even if it was the family business. Besides, she'd grown tired of trying to earn her dad's approval. She wasn't good enough, so why bother trying?

And now she found herself on another impossible ledge, in front of a man who had broken her heart. Was this God's way of making sure she didn't hold bitterness in her heart? *If I forgive him, Lord, can we speed things up and get me out of here?*

She'd *thought* she'd already forgiven him, though. He still looked like the young man she'd once known so well. His golden hair was cropped close to his forehead instead of thick and wild, and the hazel eyes still held the same mysterious intensity. She never could guess what he was thinking.

How many years had it been since he'd betrayed her family? But he'd rescued her today and put himself in danger. When he'd realized the knots would drag them both down, he'd wanted her to save herself. He wasn't supposed to be here, either. Idaho wasn't part of his life plan. There had to be a story there.

The static of a speaker caught her attention and Jackie held a warning finger to her lips. The acoustics in the canyon were amazing, and she didn't want to risk giving their location away. She shifted, pressing her back against the rock wall. Shawn followed her example, though his right eyebrow seemed to be frozen in a questioning arch. The cliff above their heads jutted out like a roof. She hoped, given the angles, that they were shielded from view.

"Update?" a voice asked through the phone.

"What should I tell him? Think we got them?" The man's deep voice carried. Jackie had a hard time telling with the wind, but she was fairly certain that was the murderer.

"I can't see that far down with the sun setting, and I'm not willing to get any closer to the edge," another man remarked. "Tell him we're done."

The static returned. "All clear here," the deep voice said. "Over."

"Over," came the reply.

"If they aren't dead, they will be once the storms hit," the other man said.

"Let's finish the job and then I'll make sure of it later. Come on."

The ATV engines roared again. Only after the noise faded into an eerie silence did Jackie feel safe enough to speak again in a whisper. "How are we going to get out of this, Shawn? Did you hear them? They're going to check back to make sure they finished the job."

"I don't understand anything yet." Shawn turned to face her. "Who are they?"

"All I know is I witnessed a murder at the geothermal plant site. I don't think they want me to be able to tell the police." She waited a beat for some kind of response, but he seemed deep in thought. "They want me dead, Shawn."

"What?" His eyes widened. "Is that why he was chasing you?" He exhaled. His expression changed as if he'd suddenly put on a law enforcement hat. "Start from the beginning. What exactly happened?"

"I heard one of those men—I think the one with the deeper voice—arguing with an employee. At least he drove a snowmobile and carried a clipboard, so I'm assuming he's staff. The employee was upset with the man about a detective." She pointed to her shoulder. "The guy killed the employee then. Injected him with something."

Shawn paled and his gaze flickered to her hands. He took off his gloves. "Put these on."

She hesitantly accepted. Her fingers felt like icicles, freezing and brittle, as if any impact could break them. "Thank you. As soon as my hands warm up a bit I'll give them back." She closed her eyes in relief, even though the pain of splinters still begged for attention.

"The good news is that what you've described hasn't included a gun."

She opened her eyes and realized the significance of Shawn's words. "He wants to make the murders look like they're accidents."

"Well, we don't know that, but the injection and push-ing a truck off the cliff seems to lean that way. We can hope they aren't armed." He lifted the hem of his jacket and checked the belt at his waist. "We may have lost my satellite phone, but at least my gun holster is made of sturdier stuff."

"Was that what I knocked out when I grabbed you?" She cringed. "I'm so sorry."

"I can't complain. You were saving my life," he said.

"Which was only necessary because you were sav-ing mine." The setting sun cast a shadow on his strong jawline. She gestured at his holster. "Is it loaded?"

"At all times." He leaned forward, ever so slightly. "They were right about one thing. If we don't find a way out of here, the blizzard heading our way will hit us."

"Blizzard?" To reach that classification, temperatures had to drop below ten degrees and sustained wind gusts would be over thirty-five miles an hour, at minimum. Not to mention the massive amounts of snow usually involved. In other words, they were facing the possibility of death either way they looked at it. "I don't know if my boss ever got my text, but I'd told him not to expect to hear from me until Monday night at the earliest." Six nights in winter conditions… They wouldn't be able to survive.

"What about friends?" Shawn asked. "Relatives? Anyone expecting you or know where you've gone?"

She opened her mouth to reply and stopped. She stayed busy, with a full work calendar at most times, but she rarely committed to social events. If she attended, it was always as a last-minute decision. That way she didn't disappoint anyone if it didn't work out. "I want to come, but don't count on me," she'd often say. In the early days of her career, she'd made the excuse because she didn't know when a story would demand her attention. Now she didn't work under such short deadlines, but she'd grown accustomed to the benefit of no expectations.

In fact, she'd asked her cousin if it was okay to be flexible about her coming to the wedding. Since it was a family-style dinner reception, her cousin was fine with it. Even her parents didn't know she was coming. Jackie thought it'd be a fun surprise and then she could join them for Christmas.

Now the plan seemed more foolish than fun. No

one would miss her presence for days. And in front of Shawn, admitting that proved hard to do. "No," she said softly. "No one will be expecting me until Monday night. What about you?"

Shawn blew out a long breath, the air producing a giant cloud of fog in front of him. "I've already put notices on the exits to the land. We close in the event of severe weather. The radars said multiple winter storms will hit before the blizzard camps out here a few days."

She shivered and her teeth chattered, not so much from the cold, but from despair. The thought of having to survive in a blizzard on a ledge in the mountains with her ex-boyfriend was too much. "Wait. Won't they be worried and look for your truck if you don't call in?" She pointed at the logo on his jacket. "Surely the Bureau has a helicopter. They'd spot the vehicle immediately."

"Jackie, I'm responsible for four million acres. Spotting my broken truck hundreds of feet below—in a relatively thin canyon—is not as easy as you might think. Especially if it starts snowing." His shoulders slumped. "Besides, I already told the field office I would make sure the field archaeologist was done taking samples for the day and escort him out of the park before heading home." He spotted the question in her eyes before she could ask. "But I didn't let the archaeologist know. He's probably gone for the day by now."

He leaned his head back and sighed. "I was also keeping a lookout for a missing hiker, but his brother claims he's in a different region than mine. The point is that I've signed off for the day."

"Anyone in—" She hesitated for a second. "Is there

someone in your life who will send out the dogs if you don't get home?"

He cleared his throat. "No."

So he was single, too. Not important given the circumstances, but she had so many questions. She told herself it was the nature of her job rather than interest in him, but she should still slow down. "Thank you again for saving my life." Her throat tightened. "And I'm sorry I got you into this."

"It's my *job* to save people," he answered.

The message seemed loud and clear. She shouldn't attach any feelings to the fact he'd saved her life. It was business as usual, for him. "Ranger Saves Reporter," she muttered.

Both his eyebrows jumped.

"That's what the headline will probably say. When we get out of here," she added. Positive thinking was the first step to survival. "Any food or water in your pack?"

He shook his head solemnly. "Everything in my survival kit was in the truck."

Her heart still pounded at an uncomfortable speed. She knew what needed to be done but wanted time to gather her wits. Out-of-the-box solutions often came with a little reflection. Except she could feel Shawn's gaze, studying her. "I really didn't expect to see you here," she said.

He barked a laugh. "You and me both. Possibly the understatement of the year." He offered her a kind smile. "BLM law enforcement rangers usually get stationed in California to start. It's a competitive field, but I'd been waiting for a spot in Idaho for a few years."

"My dad was under the impression you had no intention of ever coming back." She closed her mouth in a tight line. She shouldn't have even said that much. Shawn had been their neighbor and probably spent more time at her house than his own. He had been best friends with her brother, and they'd all grown up together. Her parents had practically treated him like an adopted son until graduation night, the last night they'd seen him.

His neck reddened and the little muscle in his jaw flexed. He avoided looking in her direction. "My mom remarried and moved to Sun Valley. I thought it'd be nice to be in the same state again."

"Sun Valley? Wow. A resort town." The beautiful and expensive vacation area was roughly four hours away in her estimate.

"She's living the life she always wanted. I'm happy for her." This time a small, genuine smile appeared, but it vanished the moment another breeze whistled past. "We can't afford to wait here until help arrives, Jackie."

"I know." She sagged, not fully recovered from the trauma of believing she was about to fall to her death. And when Shawn said her name, he exposed an internal vulnerability she didn't realize she still had. He knew her, and while she'd changed a lot over the years, her weaknesses were still there. "I haven't done this type of thing in ages, and my arms…"

He looked over her face. "Are you hurt?"

"No. Forget it." She didn't want to whine, and his close attention wasn't helping her heart rate normalize. She worked out every other day, but she never pushed herself to the extent needed for survival skills.

Her muscles hadn't felt this depleted since she was a teenager.

A shadow moved over the crevice. The sun began its disappearing act behind the foothills at an alarming rate. Soon, they'd have no choice at all. "Okay, let's say we figure out a way down. Then what?"

The creases in his forehead deepened for a moment. "There's an extra satellite phone kept in the archaeologist trailer. If we can make it to the trailer tonight, I'm sure we can get picked up before the storm hits. If not, at least we'd have some shelter for the night."

"Yeah, that sounds wonderful, but how do we go about that? Looks like we have at least a five-hundred-foot drop to go, and the rocks look too slick to climb down by hand."

"It's too bad that man didn't run your snowmobile off on the other side of the canyon."

She couldn't stop from rolling her eyes this time. "Oh, well, I'll try to make my imminent death more convenient next time."

He laughed and pointed directly across from them. "There's a closed trail on that side that leads up and out into the forest—dangerous to the novice but still usable."

Hope surged. If there was a trail, then maybe they really had a chance of getting out and calling for help. "Okay, so all we have to do is get five hundred feet down as darkness closes in on us. Without dying first."

Shawn recognized the frustration in her tone. She blew her dark hair out of her face once more. He had a feeling she did it without thinking, but it gave him an excuse to really study her features. She turned and he averted his eyes from her face. Her navy peacoat had scuffs and bits of bark stuck to it, as well as a white stain on the hem edging that looked fresh.

She sighed. "We have to do something I haven't done in over a decade." She put her hands on her hips. "We have to ask the question we were trained to ask during every survival training."

He almost groaned aloud. His memories of Jackie brought him regret, but they weren't unpleasant. Her dad, a man he'd once considered his greatest role model, had erased every good memory when he'd shoved a finger into Shawn's chest and told him he never wanted to see his face again.

But now he was a trained law enforcement ranger, although he'd not been without his satellite phone as backup for ages. Still, he didn't need to go back to basics. "I really don't think that's necess—"

"Here goes." Jackie straightened with a nod. "What would Wolfe Dutton do?"

The name alone caused the back of his shoulders to tense. "He's *your* dad. I think you can answer that question better than I can."

She studied the rock wall as if she'd suddenly gained new perspective. "You have more rope in the bag with you?"

He twisted and pulled the bag off his back. "A two-hundred footer, but we have no way of using it to rappel down without a way to link the harness to the rope. We're also without installed anchors for climbing." He unzipped the bag to show her his measly backup gear.

She pulled his gloves off and opened her palm.

"Didn't Dad or Eddie ever teach you how to rappel when you only have a rudimentary rope and two carabiners?"

He gaped. She couldn't be serious. Off a twenty-foot hill, sure, but jumping down a canyon? "No," he finally answered. "But your brother always said Wolfe taught you more than he ever taught Eddie."

"I don't believe that for a minute." She took the rope from him and didn't waste a minute tying knots in strategic locations. "I suppose he treated us differently, but I can see plenty of benefits that Eddie had that I didn't. I also watched the television show. I think I was the only one in the family that actually did. It was easy to get my dad talking about everything behind the scenes. Eddie was just too busy with his video games." She gave Shawn a side-glance. "With you."

He shrugged. "We had galaxies to save."

"Well, I'm sure Eddie was with me when he taught us this." Her hands moved fluidly, wrapping and pulling, despite the redness evident on her knuckles. She always talked rapidly when she wanted to avoid something that stressed her out. At least some things never changed.

She tied the last knot and beamed. "If I could figure out the reasoning behind why he did things a certain way, then I could remember the technique. I suppose that's why I'm a journalist. I can't stop asking questions."

Any warmth left in his body seemed to drain away. "You're a reporter? For a TV station?"

She tilted her head and eyeballed him with suspicion. "No, I mean I used to be. But now I write for the *Idaho Gazette*, based in Boise."

"Oh." Maybe her coming here was a coincidence, but he had to be sure. "Then why are you here?"

She moved to tie the rope concoction into her make-shift harness. "My editor sent me to cover a story about sabotage at the geothermal plant being built. Surely you know about that. It's just a mile or so north of here. Probably part of your four million acres?"

Of course *he* knew about it. "But how'd your editor hear about that?" He tried and failed to keep his voice light.

She squinted at him. "Why? I never knew you had an investigative streak in you."

"You like to talk when you're stressed about something. I'm just making conversation."

"It's been years since we've known each other, Shawn," she said quietly. "You don't know if I still do that. People change. And this seems too pointed for conversation."

"Fair enough. The sabotage wasn't public knowledge. Please just tell me, Jackie."

She handed him an end of the rope and indicated he should tie it to his harness as she answered. "A former coworker is the news director at Channel 7. He sometimes passes along nibbles they won't be using. This was an anonymous tip they didn't have space to pursue." She pursed her lips for a second. "Why? Was the sabotage confidential?"

His gut churned and threatened to cause problems. He shook his head. He had to come clean. "You're here because of me."

"What are you talking about?" She stared at him, her eyes wider than he'd ever seen. She dropped the rope and held up a finger. "If you think *I* followed you here as some ridiculous ploy to get your attention, you are sorely mistaken. And if you think I've been keeping tabs on you all these years, you're also wrong. I was genuinely surprised to find you here. In fact, you can rest assured that I've gotten over you, utterly and completely. I haven't given you a thought since—"

He held up his hands. If there were more room on the ledge he would've taken a giant step back. "Jackie, that's not what I meant." His eyebrow rose, replaying her words. "Not a *single* thought?" He couldn't say the same about her, but that wasn't fair. "No, don't answer that. I meant that it's my fault that you're here. Is this off the record?"

Her shoulders sagged. "I get so tired of that question. If we are talking about personal matters, you don't even need to worry."

"But I think this is about your story. Off the record," he said again, despite her exasperated sigh. "I called in a tip about the sabotage at the geothermal site."

"You did *what*?" Her eyes softened. "To get me to come out here?"

"No." He blew out a breath of frustration. He was handling this poorly. "A few days ago, I called the TV news station. I didn't know it would end up in your hands, and honestly, I didn't think they would send someone out all this way to report on it. I thought they might call the BLM Idaho communication director, get some phone interviews, slap a stock image of the area on the screen and give it a ten-second sound bite. Once the issue became public, more resources would be sent."

She stared at him, her eyes widening. "First, that's not how this works. Public lands are a hot topic in Idaho. Many think they should be returned to the state."

Shawn shook his head and gestured past the thick patch of evergreen trees to the south of the gorgeous mountain backdrop. "Much of this is considered un-inhabitable. The fact of the matter is the state couldn't afford to take care of it. We lease the resources and the state gets half the proceeds. It's a nonissue."

"That's not the point. If there's potential for a hot breaking story, they send a journalist." She tapped her index finger to her chest, and then tilted her head as if to study his reaction for a second. "Why were you so worried about the sabotage? Surely you took it to your supervisors first?"

"Still off the record?"

She rolled her eyes. "Yes."

His face stung, likely more from embarrassment than the cold. "I wondered if the saboteurs knew something that the impact and feasibility report didn't cover." He suddenly felt very awake, having said it aloud.

"Like?"

He grimaced at the dimming light. They still needed to get all the way down and then climb all the way back on the other side's trail. "Let's get moving and I'll tell you on the way down."

She bit her lip with a nod. "I suppose I might be procrastinating." She took a deep breath. "Okay. We take the center of the rope and wrap around this boulder that juts out. We tie eight gathering knots. One of us goes down first and finds a suitable anchor before we stop. The other person starts working their way down, pulling on the left side of the rope until one half of the knot pops, then the right half of the rope until it pops. You're essentially untying each knot until you're out of rope."

His gut flipped at the thought.

"It's imperative you keep the ropes balanced until you reach me," she added.

"No wiggling," he said, trying to keep his voice light.

"And remember it's important that you count correctly."

"Or the knots will all come loose and we'll plummet to our deaths. Got it."

Her grave expression left nothing to imagination. "I'm sorry. That's the only way I can think of to get the rope back down to us so we can retie and start again." She shook her head. "How about you go first? I'll do the untying of the knots on the way down."

"Absolutely not." He wouldn't give her the riskiest part of the job. As he'd just told her, it was his job to rescue, not the other way around.

"Shawn, I've never done this technique on my own, and I'm not even sure I remember it right."

He sneaked a peek over the ledge once more. Five hundred feet was a low estimate. Even if her technique worked, they would have to find rocks or branches that weren't slippery from the snow and could hold their weight at least four more times. He grimaced. "I'd rather die trying than wait for a blizzard and a murderer to finish us off."

She removed her cross-body purse and handed it to him. "Could you put that in your pack?"

He did so as she removed her navy peacoat, revealing a gray ribbed sweater and tan dress pants that appeared way too thin to be out in the elements for long. Even her suede boots looked like they were more for fashion than function. She tossed the coat over the ledge.

"What'd you do that for?" His voice rose louder than he intended. Hopefully the wind carried his outburst the opposite direction of wherever those men went.

Her teeth began to chatter, but she threw the end of the rope over her shoulder and around the inside of her left leg. "It would be too easy for the coat to catch on the rope, and it's too big to fit in your small pack. I'm hoping it'll be waiting for me at the bottom. Your coat is short enough that it should be fine, but—"

"Take mine, then." He went to unzip but she held her hand out.

"No. Your arms are too long and it would impede my ability to handle the rope. But now that I think about it, you should put your gun and—is that a Taser?—in your pack."

"Standard issue," he simply replied. He did as she asked without argument in hopes they could get her down and warm again as fast as possible. The temperature hovered in the low thirties, but the wind made it feel colder. "At least put my gloves back on."

She accepted with a sheepish smile and replaced her holds on the rope. "Guide my descent slowly." Her head vibrated with shivers. "But not too slowly. I'll yell out when I find the next place to anchor." She closed her eyes as if lifting up a prayer, then flashed him a quick smile and leaned back until she fell off the ledge.

THREE

The work of going down a cliff without proper equipment made the descent tedious and grueling. They worked together without dialogue, communicating only what they needed to. Shawn counted aloud each time a side of the rope lost its tension, meaning it'd given up half a knot.

Thus far, their plan had worked. She'd found another foothold to balance on while he descended to join her. The muscles in between her shoulder blades were screaming, though.

On the fifth time repeating the descent—since the drop turned out to be a lot deeper than she'd estimated—his foot slipped off a rock hold. She could feel the popping of the knots within the rope as it vibrated from above. He was descending too fast. And there was nothing she could do about it.

He tapped his feet against the wall as he tried to catch onto something, attempting to slow down, but he dropped down past her.

"No!" She reached for him, letting go of the rope with her right hand, a disastrous decision. She no longer had anything to hold her steady. She dropped like a stone.

Right onto his stomach.

He groaned and rolled to the side.

She fell to her knees on the snow-covered ground and spun around. "I'm so sorry." She studied him for broken bones in the dim light. "Are you okay?"

His frown shifted into a beaming smile, and he patted his jacket. "Padding." He laughed. "Good thing we were so close to the ground." His smile was contagious.

She leaned back onto her heels. "I can't believe we did it." The physical effort had caused a sweat, despite her lack of a coat, but she was ready to find it before hypothermia became a risk. And now that the sun had almost disappeared, the temperatures would plummet well below freezing. Only, she didn't see her coat anywhere.

Shawn caught her gaze and rose to his feet. "I was afraid of that. The wind might've caught it like a kite in the canyon." He removed his coat. "I insist this time."

Underneath, he wore a long-sleeve button-up shirt the same shade of khaki as his official jacket, with dark brown pants and trail shoes. She'd never imagined he'd gained so much muscle after high school, but all evidence of childhood had left his face. His broad shoulders strained against the seams.

He draped his coat over her shoulders before she could object. Even more than the gloves he'd loaned her, the coat radiated with his warmth. Except the sudden heat served to inform her internal thermostat what she'd been through. Her teeth chattered. She couldn't seem to get warm enough.

Shawn put his holster back on, complete with gun on one side and Taser on the other. He pulled out his cell phone and grimaced. "Still no signal. I'm going to turn it to airplane mode and so should you. The battery drains faster if it's constantly searching. We'll try again once we reach the top."

She checked. Sure enough, no signal.

He stuffed the rope into his backpack before he straightened. "Come on. The light is almost completely gone. The trail should be somewhere nearby." He stopped at a set of boulders on the other side of the canyon. "Found it."

Her eyes followed the steep incline of the trail that barely made an indentation in the side of the dirt and rock wall. No wonder they'd closed it off.

"I think we should stay close. The light is dim and I don't want any missteps." He reached out his hand for her to hold. "Just in case."

"If I fall off, I don't want to take you with me. You broke my fall last time, but if it'd been far—"

"I'm the law of the land around here." He winked and she knew he wasn't serious, but the edge to his voice made it clear he wasn't in a mood to argue. "Let's get to safety."

She placed her left hand in his and followed him. He had a giant sweat stain in the middle of his back, evidence of the physical strain he'd endured. "Think I can use my phone light to—"

"If we're dealing with a murderer, I don't think we can risk drawing any attention to our location, especially down here without any camouflage." As if to highlight his point, the sound of engines carried with the wind. Above, somewhere on the top of the cliff, two beams of light bounced around, shining into the darkening skies. The lights seemed to be from a bigger vehicle than an ATV or snowmobile, though.

"Do you think they're friend or foe?" he asked.

"Well, either way, we should get up and find out. Right?"

He turned around to face her and reached for her other hand. "Hang on. There are some iffy spots, and with the snow…" His voice trailed off as he helped her up and over a boulder until they were standing side by side again. He dropped her other hand and turned back to the trail. His pace was fast enough that she struggled a little to keep up.

"You should take the gloves back, at least," she said. "I've got your coat."

"I'm fine." His foot pushed through the snow a little too forcefully and she could feel his balance shake. She squeezed his hand tighter and pulled back as hard as she could. He found his footing but still she didn't let go. The way his fingers trembled revealed just how close he'd been to falling.

"Snow bridge," he finally said. "Looked like part of the ledge but really was just air. I'll take it a little slower now." He took a bigger step, this time testing for firmness before he pulled her over the hole.

They walked in silence for a few minutes. She hated to admit she hadn't changed, but he'd been right earlier. She needed to talk. If her mind and mouth stayed busy, the physical reactions to stress were kept to a minimum. "You said you were worried the saboteurs knew something that the impact and feasibility report didn't cover. Why?"

"More a precautionary action than a concern. There's been a problem or two in other states. Not ours. In every organization there is a bad apple, and sometimes big money can entice."

"That's a really vague answer, Shawn."

"Maybe, but you're a reporter, and I happen to like my job—well, part of it."

He was scared she would make him lose his job? She would've thought he'd known her better. Though, admittedly, she'd argued that he didn't have the right to say he knew her. Sometimes finding the truth proved exhausting. "Fine. Officially, until we find safety, everything you say is off the record."

He exhaled. "When sabotage happens you can't help but wonder why. So I started to wonder if there really was a plan to address the needs of the Greater Sage-Grouse, like the geothermal plant impact report indicated. Otherwise, why would environmental groups get involved?"

"Are sage-grouse like little birds?"

"Well, they can get about two feet tall, but yeah." He shrugged. "Part of my job is understanding the wildlife habitat of the land. Sage-grouse are a big deal in this area."

"Why are you so sure an environmental group is responsible?"

"This type of sabotage… It's mild and aimed at the construction."

"I wouldn't call murder *mild.*"

He was silent for a second. "A valid point, but we

don't know if the sabotage and murder are connected, do we? The saboteurs didn't touch a thing while the control building and the air-cooler structure assembly was being built. The only thing left is pad preparation for the drilling rigs to be assembled. The sabotage started when they got closer to the grouse habitat. It just makes sense to suspect it's all about the grouse."

"Did it make sense to your supervisors?"

He shrugged but kept his face forward, watching the trail carefully as they climbed. "When I told my boss, he didn't think the sabotage warranted extra resources."

"So you suspect he plays a part in this?"

His spine straightened for a second. "To be fair, he doesn't have much to work with. We are notoriously short-staffed."

"Then what's the big deal about this kind of grouse?"

"People travel from all around the world to witness the famous male courtship call. The male bird changes shape and the call is kind of comical, but their numbers have decreased at an unprecedented rate. Since they're an umbrella species—"

"What does that mean?"

"Saving their habitat would mean we're also saving a bunch of other species that rely on the same habitat."

A howl broke the stillness and sent a chill up her spine. Other howls and yips followed, some long and soulful, others more like a pack of teenage girls screaming. They carried on for a few minutes, and she didn't bother trying to speak over their party of sorts.

"They're just dogs," Shawn said.

"Yeah, dogs that can eat you."

Maybe she found coyote packs a little scary, but logically, she knew there was minimal risk. She didn't want to think on the subject much longer, though. Darkness was closing in fast. "So you called in the sabotage tip because you wanted to keep the government accountable," she said instead. "I can get behind that. We *all* need accountability. It's why I believe in my job."

"Without enough manpower to protect the land and find out for myself, I had to know. If the mitigation plan for the grouse was working, then why would environmentalists see the need to sabotage?"

She mulled over his words. "I can't let myself make assumptions when writing a story, but your answer is better than I got from anyone at the plant. You seem to know this area well."

He took an unusually long stride on a steep decline and turned to help her, with both hands again, to make the same climb. He held both of her gloved hands for an extra second before he smiled and turned back to the trail. "I've always liked the wilderness, you know that. I enjoy my job—well, except for the law enforcement part."

"I have to say that, given a murderer is after me, I don't find your honesty to be very encouraging at the moment." She tried to use a teasing lilt, but the incline made her breathing a little strained.

He shook his head. "Just because I don't enjoy it doesn't mean I'm not good at my job." He turned and smiled. "And you're clearly good at yours, asking all the right questions."

"I'm glad you think so because I have one more question."

He turned and pointed. "Go ahead. I think we're almost to the top."

She hesitated, but the past kept flooding her brain with questions she might be able to finally put to rest. In high school, she'd dated Shawn in secret to avoid her twin brother, Eddie, making things all weird. The night of Shawn and Eddie's graduation, they'd gone to a party they should never have attended. Eddie had left intoxicated, driving Shawn's car.

The last time she'd seen Shawn was in a hospital hallway where she waited while her parents stayed with Eddie, who was unconscious with a broken back and a poor prognosis. Eddie had managed to prove the doctors wrong, though. Two years later he had fully healed and worked his way back to full functionality. Not that Shawn had ever bothered to find out.

He hadn't so much as said goodbye.

She should leave the issue alone, but her heart and mind refused to quiet. Now was her chance to find out the whole truth. "Why'd you leave?"

Shawn's heart beat harder as the trail turned into a steeper, thinner incline. Jackie's question made his head hurt. Part of him had wanted her to ask, to get everything out in the open, but the other wanted the past to stay buried deep.

"I would've forgiven you." Jackie's voice was soft. "I mean, I did anyway—it just took a little longer since I had to forgive you for leaving like that, too."

His jaw tensed. He shouldn't have needed to ask forgiveness in the first place. What he had really needed was someone to be on his side. It wasn't his fault Eddie had sneaked off and played a drinking game. Everyone assumed Shawn had known Eddie had been drinking when he'd taken his keys.

Even with the fabric of the gloves separating their touch, he wanted to let go of Jackie's hand. He took another step up the path. Duty kept his grip firm and secure. He would get her to safety. "If I had to do it all over again…" He had hoped saying something like that would put a quick and easy end to the subject, but he wasn't sure how to finish the sentence.

"What? What would you do different?"

Honestly, he didn't know. Each time he replayed the sequences of that night, he still wouldn't have had the knowledge that Eddie had been drinking, so he didn't see how any of it was in his control. If the night happened all over again, Eddie *still* would have taken his keys and ended up in the hospital, and Wolfe would still say he never wanted to see Shawn's face again. Jackie probably didn't know that tidbit, but he wasn't sure what good it would do if she did.

"I…I'd say goodbye," he finally answered. For that, he truly did regret. But he'd never forget the disgust and accusation in her eyes that night. Between her, Wolfe and the entire town, Shawn had endured shame that he didn't deserve yet could never fully erase.

He took his eyes off the trail for a second to gauge their progress. Three more steps and they'd reach higher ground. The cold had begun to seep past his defenses. He wouldn't ask for his coat back, though. He just needed to get his bearings and get them to that trailer. Walking through the snow that already had several inches built up would take a good half hour at minimum to go a single mile, though.

He reached the top and pulled her the rest of the way up to him with a final heave. Directly above them, the stars and the moon had brightened the darkness. He glanced down and could still see the hurt in Jackie's face. She knew he wasn't telling her the full story, but he wasn't ready.

He turned and trudged toward the edge of the forest. He glanced at his phone with the light on dim and pulled up the compass. "If we go due southeast, I think we'll run into the trailer."

"How many miles?"

He dreaded that question. "I'm…I'm not sure. Five?" It could be as many as ten, though. He wasn't sure now that he couldn't see where they were exactly. He'd never traveled there on foot.

Headlights swung to the east, one from a truck and another from what looked like a snowmobile. He pulled Jackie behind the closest evergreen tree to stay hidden from sight.

"Are those ATVs with the truck?"

"Looks like only a snowmobile. I didn't see an ATV."

"So maybe it's good guys," she whispered.

"Maybe." He reached for his holster out of instinct. The snowmobile took off again, revving off into the distance, but the truck headlights stayed on, as if stuck within the grove of trees. "Still, they look at least a mile or so away."

She peeked around the tree.

His muscles tightened as he tried his best to not shiver. The temperature dipped faster than expected and his back was still damp from the exertion. The wind howled past them. Thankfully, it hadn't started snowing yet. Fresh snow on top of the packed snow would make the journey even slower. Hiking in the dark, without so much as the use of a flashlight, was foolish. He didn't know this terrain well enough by foot to know all the dangers. What if there was another snow bridge?

"I think we might have to consider finding shelter for the night. This is the point where your dad would stop and make a snow cave, right?"

"Yeah, well, Dad had two other people helping him shovel so it wouldn't take eight hours. Plus, what if we don't give the snow enough time to harden and those trees get an extra boost of wind and dump enough snow on it to collapse, trapping us?" She spoke extra fast, probably to keep her teeth from chattering.

"At this rate, I'm a little concerned that we won't make it to that trailer tonight."

She gave him a side look. "Your turn." She took off the coat and shoved it in his arms. "Hurry before I change my mind. You can't rescue me if I have to drag you somewhere, and I'm pretty sure starting a fire right now would send a signal to those men that we're still alive."

He begrudgingly took the coat, determined only to wear it for a few minutes at most. "Let's keep moving, then, and see if it's friend or foe inside that truck."

He tripped over one of the many rocks and roots hiding underneath the snow. The progress proved slower than he feared. Jackie didn't complain, though. He counted silently to 120 and returned the coat to her. She raised an eyebrow but accepted. On and on they went sharing the coat back and forth until they got within a hundred yards of the red pickup truck.

"I know that truck." He could never forget, really. He *knew* that guy was the one who had dug up the wheel ruts left by the Oregon Trail pioneers, but he had no proof. "Darrell Carrillo. He's a metal detectorist, but the worst kind. He's also the hiker that's been missing. He wasn't supposed to be here." But that figured.

"So if he has a truck, maybe he just got lost?" She huffed. "But then why would the snowmobile lead him into the trees? Shawn, we have to assume he's in league with the man who tried to kill me."

He wanted to think of an innocent reason to explain the truck being in the forest, but his interactions with the man led him to believe otherwise. "Maybe." When they reached the small clearing within the trees, the lights took on an ominous glow. The truck appeared to have slammed into a tree.

Nothing about the day had made sense except for the constant current of danger. So while his normal course of action would be to rush to see if there was anyone injured inside, apprehension filled his core. He held a hand out to Jackie. "Do me a favor and stay back while I find out what's going on."

He placed one hand on his weapon and the other hand on the back of the truck, working his way forward. In the driver's seat sat the missing hiker, his forehead leaning on top of the steering wheel.

Shawn surveyed the surroundings, his hand on his

gun. No one else seemed anywhere close. The snow-mobile tracks headed southeast, in the same direction of the path the construction workers would've used.

"Is everything okay?" Jackie asked, peeking out from her hiding place behind another tree.

He opened the driver's door and the stench of alcohol wafted past him. "Definitely not okay," he said. He placed two fingers on the man's neck. No pulse. He moved to check the wrist, just in case there was any hope. "I don't think he's going to hurt you."

Jackie stepped out into the open. "Oh? So it's a friendly hiker?"

"Not exactly friendly, but we did find him." He exhaled. "Unfortunately, he's dead."

FOUR

Jackie looked away from the man hunched over the wheel.

Cold. That foremost thought played on repeat and numbed her mind, even when presented with such shocking news.

The trees surrounding them gave them a little protection but not enough to hold the wind back. Although she was wearing Shawn's coat, her jaw quivered and every muscle vibrated.

Shawn took out his phone and grimaced. "If my fingers would cooperate, that would be nice."

"What are you doing?" She came closer—the last thing she wanted to do, as she could no longer avoid the sight of the hiker. At least there was no blood.

Shawn grunted and seemed to take a lot of effort to get his hand to stop trembling enough to touch a small symbol on his phone screen. "I just want to turn the flash off. The headlights may still be on, but if there are sudden flashes of light from my phone, we might get our unwelcome visitors back to investigate."

The light from the inside of the cab seemed dim

but illuminated Shawn enough that she could see his lips had taken on a decidedly bluish tint. "We need to get warm, Shawn." They were running out of time before hypothermia became a risk. The wet spot on the back of his shirt was a surefire recipe for it. She moved to take the coat off. It was long past time to give it back to him.

"No. Keep it on." He pressed his lips together in a firm line, determination lining his features. "I have to move him."

"The body?" She couldn't keep the horror out of her voice but realized why he'd decided on the course of action. Trucks had heaters. The accident didn't look too bad, structurally, for the truck. The headlights were on, so the truck still had a working battery. They could probably drive back to the road and make it to civilization within a couple of hours. She'd find a hotel with a fireplace and hot cocoa and one of those thick terry cloth robes. Her shoulders rose to her ears, bracing against the wind. They just needed to get inside that truck.

"Yes. I have to move him. That's why I need to take photos." He moved his phone in several different angles around the body. "I hope the lighting is decent enough."

Crime scene photos, she finally realized. "You don't think his death was an accident."

His eyes darted to her and back to the phone. "That's not my call to make. It *appears* to be an accident. If I were an optimistic man, I would hope that the people on the snowmobile witnessed the accident and are heading back to civilization to call it in. If that's the case, our best chance for survival is to stay put and be found along with…" He bent at an odd angle to take more photos of the man's shoes near the pedals. "Along with him," he finally said. "But we investigate every death, accidental or not."

Shawn used to be an optimist. At least, that was how she'd always thought of him. The thought jarred her. They'd been apart for over a decade, but she'd still known him longer than she hadn't. People changed faster once they were adults, though.

"But where will we put him?" she asked. "I suppose the cold will help preserve the body." The branches of the trees surrounding them rustled with the breeze. She knew better than most what lurked in the shadows. "Won't animals…?" She didn't want to speak the question aloud, either. Law enforcement wouldn't be able to properly investigate the man's death if wild scavengers found him first. The haunting howl of the coyotes sounded again, confirming her thoughts.

"Thankfully, we have his keys." Shawn leaned over the man. He removed the key from the ignition but left the headlights on. He stomped over to the trunk of the covered cab. His entire hand shook as he tried to insert the key into the lock. "Getting them to work is another matter."

"If you're not going to take the coat back, at least let me help you." She took the key from his hand and unlocked it. The back opened to reveal a metal detector, a duffel bag, a jug of partly frozen water, a wool blanket, an emergency car repair kit and a backpack. A backpack usually contained snacks if someone was out hiking in the wilderness. "Shawn…"

"Go ahead and take stock of supplies, but please tell me the contents before you use anything."

He disappeared back to the front of the truck. She emptied the emergency car kit for its first-aid kit, emergency blanket and the day/night flare in case they needed it for a fire starter, but she left behind the jumper cables. The main zippered compartment of the backpack revealed beef jerky, a tuna packet, trail mix, four disposable water bottles that were on their way to being frozen but were still liquid, and a box of chocolate-covered almonds. "Oh, you were a good man." Her voice wavered as she realized that their best chance of survival was now because a man had died.

"I'm not so sure about that." Shawn stomped in the snow with—she gasped—the man in question over his shoulder. He grunted and maneuvered the man off his shoulder, into his arms and inside the bed of the truck.

The man wore a short, padded coat, jeans, a cap and tennis shoes. Shawn turned the man's face away from her view so she could only see the back of his head. A kind gesture, but try as she might, she couldn't fool her mind into thinking that he was just sleeping.

The wind gusted enough to shift the truck ever so slightly to the right. Desperation for warmth kept her from crying out over the dead man. The thought jarred her. Two men had died in one day and she'd almost been added to their number. Her eyelids felt like they might freeze closed as she blinked away the hot moisture.

"I'll check this one." Shawn reached across her and unzipped the duffel bag. On top of a pile of fabrics of some sort sat metal trinkets, some covered in mud, a pair of binoculars and what looked like an arrow-head. "He definitely wasn't up to any good if this is any indication."

Underneath, the items proved more interesting. "Shawn. Are those clothes?"

He pulled out gloves, a parka, extra socks and snow pants. Shawn gave a solemn nod. "Ill-intentioned or not, he was prepared for the elements." He gestured to the backpack. "Let's take this and the duffel and see if we can get the heat on."

They closed the covered bed of the truck. The back of her neck tightened with guilt over using the dead man's truck, but they couldn't start a fire without a couple of hours of gathering supplies and fighting the wind. Even if they managed to create a spark, the smoke and flames would act as a beacon to those who'd likely killed him. They really had no other choice but to utilize the supplies.

She stuck the duffel in the back seat for easy access and slipped into the passenger side of the truck. Shawn's open door made it feel like she'd entered a wind tunnel. She bit her lip to keep from telling him to hurry up as he took more photos of the empty driver's seat and the floor. She tucked her chin deeper into the coat until he finally slipped into the driver's side. The moment he shut the door, her skin burned with a strong intensity, as if her brain finally thought it was safe to give her body permission to acknowledge the full extent of what she'd been through. No more denial to survive, to keep moving. Everything hurt.

Shawn shoved the key into the ignition. "Let's hope this works." He clicked the key over and the engine

revved to life. He flipped the thermostat to the red-
dest portion but kept the fan on low. She pulled off the
gloves and held her hands up to the air vent. Cold air
blasted, but it was warmer than outside.

Shawn twisted and contorted in his seat. "That
parka looked warm."

"You should take your coat back."

"No, this will be fine." He struggled in the small
space until he succeeded in putting on the thinner coat.
But at least it had a hood. He cleared his throat. "He
may not have been a law-abiding citizen, but I'd like
to think he would've helped us." He shrugged. "I'd
like to think that anyone would have compassion in
such conditions."

There was the Shawn she remembered, the one who
found the silver lining. Even though she knew from
covering the news for years that the sentiment wasn't
true, she remained silent. She bristled against his mention of compassion.

Now that she finally had reprieve from the wind
and cold, her mind wanted to give full attention to
the unsatisfactory answer he'd given her back on the
trail. The only thing he'd do differently all those years
ago was to say goodbye? Her throat tightened at the
thought.

What had she expected him to say? *Oh, dearest
Jackie, that night was the biggest mistake of my life. I
should've begged for your forgiveness right then because I loved you, and I've never stopped thinking
about you.*

She knew the pretend speech too well because she'd
imagined Shawn proclaiming such things on a loop in

the days after he'd left. She hadn't recalled the imaginary teenage interchange in years, though. If Shawn had actually said something similar on the trail moments ago, she might've felt more satisfied with his answer. But then what?

The question perplexed her, which probably indicated there would've been an awkward silence.

Shawn handed her a pair of wool socks. "Here."

Thoughtful gestures didn't help to put her mind to rest. Simply having dry fabric against her toes was enough to cause her eyes to well up with gratitude, but she refused to shed tears.

The air shifted. Heat!

Shawn turned the fan on full blast before she had a chance. In a few short hours, she'd be able to put all the internal drama in the back of her mind, where it belonged. Because even if Shawn had given an awesome explanation about the past, they couldn't pick up a relationship where they'd left off.

Her job was in Boise and his was hours away, in the middle of nowhere. He obviously still adored spending his time in the wild, while she refused to even camp. And how could she ever trust a man who left like that, without so much as a word? She leaned forward, anxious to focus on other things. "So can we head for the road now?"

Shawn turned to face her, his eyes widening. He stared at her for an uncomfortable few seconds, as if he expected her to remember something and speak first.

"What?"

He frowned and shook his head. "Jackie, we won't

be able to drive this anywhere. I thought you'd realized."

"Thought I realized what?" She leaned forward, peering out of the windshield. "I know the truck hit the tree, but neither looks the worse for wear. I don't think the tree will fall on us if we back away. Is it a flat tire? I'm not happy about it, but I'm capable and willing to wrestle out the spare if it means we can leave tonight."

He shook his head sadly, so she pressed on. "I'm even willing to stand outside and guide you through these trees. It shouldn't take long to get to some solid snowpack. You know the area well enough that you won't drive us off a cliff, right?"

He didn't blink. "That's not the issue."

"We can beat the worst of the storm. It hasn't even started snowing yet." Like a cruel trick, thick snowflakes floated down to the windshield. Her shoulders sagged. "I still say we can make it to civilization tonight if we try."

"The back axle, Jackie. It's broken clean in two."

Please let him be wrong. She straightened. "Are you sure? I have a bit of experience with fix—"

"I know." He gestured to her door. "Whoever drove the truck here rode right over a massive log. The truck bed is being held in place by it. My guess is they planned to park this thing elsewhere, but after the break, they made do."

She peeked at the side mirror. The right tire tilted inward at a forty-five-degree angle. She should be thankful the truck sat fully upright. There went her dreams of nice warm accommodations for the beginning of her Christmas vacation.

She opened the backpack and pulled out two granola bars. Shawn accepted one and ripped off the wrapper. He finished it in three bites. She wasn't much slower. "Why do you think they meant to park the truck elsewhere? I'm guessing you don't think he died from a heart attack. Seems to me you're implying that it's murder."

He eyed her. "This is off the record, too, but surely you noticed his smell."

"Like he'd been dunked in whiskey? Yes." If she noticed things on her own, she didn't need him to be on the record. In fact, maybe if she got the scoop on the murders, she could finally get the promotion she wanted and never have to accept stories out in the wilderness again, despite her dad being the one and only Wolfe Dutton.

"Or some sort of alcohol," Shawn said. "The front of Darrell's coat had the strongest smell, but there was no liquor bottle in the car."

"He could've finished off his drink first. Elsewhere."

"True. But then I got into the truck without having to adjust the seat." He threw a thumb over his shoulder. "Darrell was a good five inches shorter than me." He glanced down at the coat. "At least he had a long torso."

So if someone else had been driving the truck, that person most likely moved the body to the driver's-side seat and staged the death to look like a drunk-driving accident. "You're saying that we're stuck in a truck that won't drive, with a dead man in the back who may or may not have been murdered by the same man that tried to kill me—or another dangerous murderer—and all with a blizzard on the way."

He rubbed both hands together and exhaled. Despite the truck's heater, his breath still made a foggy cloud. "I'm saying it's time to accept that we're operating in survival mode."

Shawn didn't regret his words, but he wasn't sure Jackie understood the severity of their situation yet. With the park closed so close to Christmas and the impending winter storm, murderers after them or not, every decision they made from this moment on would contribute to whether they lived or died.

He opened his photo album on the phone. He'd taken over a hundred shots because he never knew what would prove to be an important detail in the light of day. He flicked to the image that still perplexed him.

"So we're here all night?" Jackie asked.

"Yes."

"Are we hoping to be rescued?"

"I think the best we can hope for is that we aren't discovered by whoever planted Darrell's body here. I assume they were trying to make it look like an accident, so it seems unlikely they'd return, but I'm ready for them if they do." He patted the holster that sat on top of the console in between their seats.

She glanced at his phone and rummaged in her pockets until she pulled out hers. "I don't suppose we have a signal."

"Sorry, no." He tilted his screen in Jackie's direction. The photo that was bothering him only included the man's black ski jacket. He pointed at the white streak on the bottom hem in the photo. "That stain looked fresh."

She had her arms wrapped around herself but leaned forward, squinting. "You think it's an important detail?"

"Probably not, but you had a very similar spot on your jacket. Of course, you'd also slid off a cliff."

"That mark wasn't from the cliff. I accidentally brushed up against something during the tour of the construction site. They use some special latex paint for extreme temperatures. Each coat takes a couple days to dry, apparently. The foreman apologized and said it only needed another hour or so to cure." She shrugged. "I chalked it up to my good timing."

"So it's possible Darrell was at the construction site, as well."

She looked upward, as if in deep thought. "I noticed he wore tennis shoes. Seemed like an odd choice of footwear to be out in this thick of snow. Especially when he'd packed boots and had a metal detector."

"There's cement paths that I assume were cleared when you took the tour today?"

"Yes. I guess if he was going to stick to the paths, that makes sense, but still seems odd." She handed him back his phone. "Why'd you imply he wasn't a good man?"

He grabbed the wool blanket they'd retrieved from the duffel and folded it into a rectangle so they could both use half if he stretched it lengthwise. "It's a felony to even keep a metal detector in your vehicle on federal lands, let alone use it. We suspected him of ruining some historic sites."

"Why was he a suspect?"

"I don't have proof, but I've seen this truck on the land before. I spotted him a couple months ago through my binoculars on my rounds, from one of the higher vantage points. He had that metal detector with him, but he got away before I was close enough to get his license plate number. When the missing person photo came through with the vehicle description, as well, I knew it was him."

"Are hikers with metal detectors common?"

"Most detectorists follow the law and only search in legal areas with permission, but there's always a few that treat it more like a moneymaking scheme than a hobby. They don't care about preserving history. They think they're entitled to do or take anything they want on federal land." He shook his head. "I'm still angry about the gouges I found on a section of the Oregon Trail. Those wagon ruts survived all this time until someone took a shovel to them. Probably all for a rusty nail."

Her forehead creased. "What did you call him?"

"Darrell?"

"No, the other thing."

"A detectorist. Someone who uses a metal detector."

"Oh. I might've filled in the blanks incorrectly." Her wide eyes turned his way. "The murder I witnessed… The man didn't actually say he was upset about a detective."

He caught on instantly. "You think you misheard?"

"He said *detect*, but he was interrupted. My brain just finished the word for him. I didn't think there could be another option, but he might've been upset about a detectorist."

Shawn knew witnesses could be unreliable for that very reason. The brain had an uncanny way of trying to help along anything that didn't make sense. "So it's possible the two men were fighting about Darrell. Especially if it turns out he'd been on the property."

"Yes. But why would they be upset? What could he have seen or found? Or maybe he was behind the sabotage, but why?" Her face was animated and a good reminder that she was a journalist.

"If we knew that, maybe we'd know why two men are dead. It's probably best to let the matter rest." His phone screen taunted him with the words *No Service* still at the top of the screen.

Even with the new information, there was nothing he could do without calling for backup. His first priority was to get Jackie to safety. The archaeologist's trailer still seemed to be the best course of action. There would be supplies, a generator and, most important, a satellite phone. "At first light, we get to that trailer."

"I'm assuming you've never hiked this route to the trailer?"

"You'd be right."

She opened the glove compartment. "Maybe the guy had a terrain map of some sort?" She searched and found nothing except the truck's manual and registration.

At least she didn't argue that they should attempt to get to the trailer after nightfall. She knew as well as he did that hiking in such conditions was a recipe for death, but it'd been over a decade since she'd practiced wilderness skills, despite her memory of rappelling knots. It took training and practice to keep the skills up to par to face whatever the wilderness threw at him. But Jackie wasn't the type of person to keep her opinions quiet. At least, she didn't used to be.

In fact, he was a little surprised she'd let the topic of his leaving town abruptly go so easily. She hadn't said another word about it since he'd answered her on the trail.

She pulled out a container of chocolate-covered almonds. "I know we should probably ration our food, but that granola bar wasn't enough for dinner. And these are my favorite." She popped one in her mouth and offered him the container.

"Since when are these your favorite?" The moment the question left his mouth, he regretted it. A moment ago he was thankful she'd let the past go, and yet he'd just invited discussion. "I only meant I thought nuts were banned at your house."

She nodded and popped another in her mouth. "My mom is allergic to peanuts and tree nuts, but as soon as I went to college, I discovered that chocolate tastes better when paired with nuts. Even the chocolate itself tastes better. I'm serious," she said. "Just let it melt in your mouth and then spit out the nut, and you'll see I'm right. Better than normal chocolate. You know what I mean? Try it."

He couldn't help but laugh. He'd forgotten how enthusiastic she could get over the small joys in life, like food. "No, thanks. That's wasting a perfectly good source of protein and fat." He took a few from the box. "How is your mom, anyway?"

Her enjoyment of the chocolate dimmed. "Do you really care enough to know?"

He'd opened the door wide for discussion and perhaps even deserved that gibe. "Of course I do."

"Sorry. That was uncalled for. She's fine. Same as always." She set the box of almonds down. "I just don't understand how you could just walk away from us if you really cared. My mom always treated you like you were part of the family. We all did. Weren't you at all curious if Eddie ever recovered? I mean, he had a broken back. For all you knew, he could've died from complications."

He straightened, suddenly warmer than he should be despite the heater's setting. Had Eddie not told her anything? "I know that it took him two years, and he drove the physical therapists crazy, but he never gave up. He worked until he was fully recovered."

Her eyes clouded. "Why— How do you know that?"

"Eddie told me. The nurse told him I kept calling to find out his status. They wouldn't talk to me, though. I finally agreed to leave my number. Eddie called back. He apologized for wrecking my car. He kept me up to date for a while. It's been several years, but I heard he's running one of the branches for your father."

"So…" She stared out the window. "You spoke to him but not me?"

Her soft voice twisted his gut in knots. He'd hurt her. How could he explain that it was for the best, without sounding like a coward? The wind railed against the trees with such intensity that a giant chunk of snow slammed on the truck's hood and shook the vehicle. "Like I said, I probably should have said goodbye before I left that night. I don't expect you to believe me, but I didn't know that Eddie had been drinking when he took my keys. And even if I had, since when has anyone been able to control Eddie?"

She raised an eyebrow and faced forward but still didn't turn his way. "That doesn't explain why you left the *way* you did. A person who is innocent doesn't just run away."

"Because your dad said he never wanted to see my face again. The whole town was against me." The words rushed out with such intensity it was as if a storm had been brewing inside of him without any forecasted warnings. The memory still stung, and the day's events just emphasized his worst fear.

The truck underscored his proclamation with an ominous ding. He searched for the source of the sound. A bright orange gas tank lit up on the dashboard. Low fuel. Great. He felt like he was disappointing, all over again, the man he'd looked up to his entire childhood. He couldn't keep Eddie safe, and now he wouldn't be able to keep Jackie safe, either.

FIVE

Jackie tapped the digital clock. It was only eight o'clock at night even though her body felt like it'd already endured a twelve-hour marathon. Everything ached. She'd only spent three horrible hours in the elements, but a very long, cold night still awaited them without fuel to keep the truck running. "It's been twenty minutes with the heater on," she said. "We need to turn the truck off."

He frowned. "I know it's a bad situation, but I think when the warning light goes on we still have a couple gallons to go on. We also want to insulate ourselves. What else is in this duffel?" He handed her the man's boots. "Think you can make these work? Your flimsy fabric ones aren't going to do you much good tomorrow."

He was right; plus, they were wet. At least the man wasn't very tall, as Shawn had pointed out. His boot size was a men's size nine. She wore a size seven in women's, so they were still a little big, but not too bad with the thick wool socks. Shawn split up the rest of the items in the duffel to carry in between the two backpacks, in preparation for their early-morning hike.

Then he stretched out the duffel bag and placed it on top of their wool blanket. "Every bit of fabric helps to keep us warm."

What she really wanted was to return to the subject of the past. Even if her father had flown off the handle at the time of Eddie's accident, couldn't Shawn understand? Her dad had been devastated when they'd been told of Eddie's injuries, and it was easier to blame someone else than his son, bloodied and bruised and waiting for surgery. All she remembered was her dad's disappointment when Shawn had left. But now she wondered if it was guilt.

She rolled her head clockwise in an attempt to stop her neck from complaining. Her muscles increasingly ached, and there was still a very long and cold night ahead.

Shawn shoved his hand deep into his backpack. "I think I have some pain reliever in here and a pair of tweezers in the first-aid kit."

He found the sample-size bottle and shook out a few pills into the palm of his hand. She took off her gloves to accept and his fingers brushed against hers. Her eyes refused to lift, refused to meet his. She wrapped her fingers around the pills and realized she'd been holding her breath. She swallowed the pills and Shawn beckoned her to show him her hands again.

She hesitantly offered her palms up. He set his phone in the cup holder so it shone enough to see and worked quickly. He cupped one hand at a time and went to work with the tweezers. She looked away. It hurt more if she thought about just how many splinters were embedded.

"If you could contact Eddie, why not me?" Her voice cracked with emotion she wasn't ready to feel.

His fingers stilled. "I guess I was scared I wouldn't be able to stay away." He set her left hand down gingerly and picked up her right. "I definitely couldn't bear seeing the way everyone would look at me in town. When people get that angry—even if they find out later they're wrong—it's hard to ever regain the same kind of relationship."

She tried her best to understand his reasoning but came up empty. "What exactly happened, Shawn?"

"There, I think I got them all."

"Thank you." She put on her gloves and took another swallow of very icy water that stung her throat.

"We were at the senior class party," he began.

"I remember. I was there." The worst part of secretly dating was that they could never attend or hang out at events together. So even though they'd dated for two years, it was easy to never get too serious.

"Yes. Eddie complained that the party was boring, so he walked off with his girlfriend. I found out later that they'd gone somewhere to do shots with some other couples." Shawn's voice took on a very monotone quality. "It was starting to get dark, but there was going to be a movie on the greens."

"We were going to sit together. By accident, of course."

His eyes shifted slightly in her direction. "Except Eddie didn't want to stay. I was in the middle of an intense discussion with some other guys about whether the Packers had deserved to win the Super Bowl and handed him the keys without a second glance."

That sounded like Eddie. "So why didn't you explain that to Dad?"

"He wouldn't hear it. He said I'd betrayed his trust and failed him." His frown intensified.

"But surely now…"

Shawn shook his head. "Eddie said your dad came around, but I never heard it straight from him. Like I said, it's been years since Eddie and I've talked."

Years. Seemed like such a waste. "But leaving was so drastic—"

"It wasn't as if anyone had my back. No one was on my side. Not even you."

"That's not fair. I didn't even know your side."

He shrugged. "You probably would've reacted the same way the town—"

"You're right it wasn't fair to blame you." Her forehead creased with a deep frown. "But I would hope you could forgive me for being in the wrong in the same way I had to forgive you for leaving without saying goodbye."

"Of course," Shawn answered, a little too quickly. "The bottom line is we never would've worked together anyway. Best to leave the past in the past." He leaned over and pointed at the pack in her lap. "Did I see beef jerky in there?"

She nodded, stunned, and tried to ignore the sudden smell of soy sauce and meat. If ever there was a clear indication of an ended conversation, asking for beef jerky had to be it. She knew all the reasons they wouldn't work *now*, but she didn't know of any reasons back then. So much of what he'd said confused her as if it held more than one meaning. Her temples issued a sharp warning pain behind her eyes of an impending headache.

"Sleep if you can," Shawn said, his brow furrowed low. "You experienced a lot of physical trauma hanging from that branch."

The pounding in her head and the soreness in her arms prevented her from asking more questions, but Jackie never let a mystery go unsolved without further investigation. She closed her eyes, just for a moment. The mysteries from the day were piling up too fast to mention. She would get to the bottom of what happened all those years ago, even if the truth meant she'd have to experience heartache all over again.

The snow had made a layer against the windshield and piled against the side windows. The seats weren't comfortable, but despite their attempts at blocking out the cold, the howling wind still slipped in and swept past his cheek. Shawn turned on the engine slightly earlier than planned. He'd been running it for roughly twenty minutes every hour to conserve their fuel. Jackie seemed to be in a fitful sleep. Blissful heat filled the cab again. The lines in her face smoothed and, thankfully, she didn't wake up.

At least the warmth had been strong enough to melt snow off the windshield and the side windows. He kept the headlights on, even now, to avoid raising suspicion should someone be watching. Under the cover of trees, there wasn't much to see except the flakes getting caught in the beam's gaze as they fell down.

Something flickered through the evergreen branches. He hunched over and squinted. Still nothing. He tried to move quietly as he grabbed the pair of binoculars he'd found in Darrell's bag.

The magnification took a few adjustments before he spotted the source of bobbing light. Men on ATVs and a snowmobile. He counted three. But what could be so important to risk riding on treacherous terrain in the middle of the snowstorm? Maybe the reason motivated the murders of two men and the attempted murder of Jackie.

They came to a stop. If he had to guess, the men had paused somewhere near the end of the crevice. A giant, high-powered beam turned on, flashing across the expanse of snow. The backlight illuminated the men as one walked forward and pointed it downward. Shawn's gut twisted. They'd said they would come back to make sure he and Jackie had died among the truck wreckage.

"Jackie, wake up." He hated to do it, but he couldn't take any chances. The men would know they weren't down there any minute and might start looking for them. "I don't think we can stay here."

She blinked and rubbed her face. "What?"

The beam bounced out of the deep pit and hit the tree line, heading straight for the truck. "Duck!"

He twisted sideways, getting his head close to the heater console while Jackie folded over, her head close to her knees. Sure enough, a second later, the light lit up the entire cab.

"But, Shawn, if they killed Darrell—"

He realized his mistake before she fully voiced it. If those men had been responsible for Darrell's death, they would've been expecting to see at least one person, albeit dead, behind the wheel of the truck.

A branch fell from the sky and hit the hood at the same time the sound of a gunshot reached his ears. Jackie flinched, a small scream filling the cab as she flung her arms over her head.

"They know we're here. They're coming for us, aren't they?"

"I'm afraid they are."

A loud crack and the windshield radiated with fractures around a circle. Shawn's head throbbed with the sound of impact. The beam still lit up the truck. He tried to contort to look upward and see if the bullet had actually made a hole, but he didn't find one. "Are you okay?"

She shivered. "No, I'm not okay! That was so close. They know, Shawn. They know."

A ping sounded again. This time a bullet went through the windshield and snapped the rear mirror in two. He narrowly missed the plastic hitting him in the forehead.

"We need to run, Shawn."

Since rescuers hadn't stumbled upon them with the headlights on, their chances of being saved now, so close to Christmas, reduced drastically. "You know the dangers of hiking in the night, and once we leave the vehicle there's no going back."

"I also know the dangers of being a sitting duck." She sat up and grabbed the backpack. The beam of light hit her straight on, and she bolted out of the truck.

Shouting could be heard, echoing through the open air. If the men hadn't known their location for sure, they knew now. The light disappeared. Engines revved.

He grabbed his pack, stepped outside and sank a good half a foot into fresh snow. The wind had stilled, and the sky, still thick with full clouds, momentarily stopped dropping flakes. He rounded the truck with loud footsteps, his knees lifting to waist level with each step. The only good news about the vehicles heading straight for them was the bullets stopping for a moment while they drove around the crevice and up the hill. But that would only last mere moments. If they were the murderers who had planted the truck here, they knew the path. They had minutes at the most to get away.

Jackie ran deeper into the trees. She halted after about ten feet and spun around. The moonlight hit her wide eyes. "Where do we hide? They'll see our footprints."

"We can't outrun them. I'm guessing the field trailer is at a forty-five-degree angle, southeast of here. Let's at least start in that direction."

"But we stay in the woods and go deeper if we can. Remember how we tripped over all those rocks and trunks on the way here?"

He picked up her train of thought almost instantly. "Dangerous for a snowmobile."

"And not a picnic for an ATV. Especially if we get near trees grouped together."

He glanced up at the moon and lifted a hand in the direction he thought they needed to go. "They'll have to track us on foot, which gives us an advantage. Stay close."

"They're getting closer."

He didn't need her reminder. Their engines increased

in volume, and by the sound of things, they'd reached the truck.

"What'd they do with the body?" a man shouted. The engines cut off. "Go in after them. They can't have gotten far."

Shawn couldn't hear the muffled reply. The trees were so thick that the men couldn't follow them on the snowmobiles, but it sounded like they were following on foot. If only they had more light. One wrong step and one of them could break a leg, fall into a hole or meet up with wild animals. The clouds shifted ever so slightly. The trees weren't as thick up ahead. The crunching of snow and branches followed them, pushing him to run faster, but he wasn't sure if Jackie could keep up. Without the promise of getting to heat, working up a sweat could mean hypothermia. Hope plummeted with each step. Their attackers had found their path. He heard it.

Jackie patted his back. He turned and found her holding up a flare. "I can distract them, while you try to take them down." She gestured to his gun.

In the night, outnumbered in manpower and ammunition, he didn't think it wise to start a shooting match, but the flare gave him an idea. "Distraction is a great idea. Not yet, though. Is it a simple road flare?"

"Day and night, handheld."

"Use the day side," he said in a quiet pant. He couldn't afford for the men to hear their plan. "At my signal, use wide circles so it fills the space, and then stick it in the snow, and stay low."

It didn't take long to find what he'd been searching for. As the tree grouping grew tighter on the south side, a large bank, covered with snow, rose up. A mix of evergreens and maples towered against the ridge, but they could still climb it. He wasn't sure what would be on the other side, though. Drop-offs were as common as trees in this section of land.

The moonlit shadows indicated the bottom of the bank was deep, somewhere between a ditch and a burrow. Running out into the open wasn't an option, so hiding in that space seemed like the smartest course of action.

The men were gaining on them by the sound of their footsteps. He pointed. "Right after you light the flare, go there." He stepped to the opposite side of the trees from where he wanted to eventually go. "Now or never."

Jackie twisted off the cap and orange smoke filled the sky. The day side of the handheld flare would produce a dense cloud of orange for at least a minute rather than the night side that burned short and bright. She didn't need to be told twice. She swirled the stick in a wide circle and the thick foliage trapped the smoke in the space.

"Drop it," he whispered. She stuck the bottom end in the snow and ran for the bank, just like he'd hoped. The smoke continued to gather and form an orange wall within the trees. He pulled his gun and shouted, "Drop your weapons! BLM ranger!" He fired his weapon into the ground, ducked and sprinted to join Jackie on the other side of the orange cloud. A barrage of bullets sounded, all aiming for the spot he'd just been standing in.

Jackie stood waiting for him just past the smoke.

He'd hoped she'd be in the hiding spot by now, but she'd picked up a fallen evergreen branch and swiped at his tracks until they reached the space together. The spot between the tree and the snowy bank proved tight. They could both fit, but would it be enough to hide?

He threw his pack into the space. Jackie took off her backpack and tossed it in, as well. He gestured for her to slide in first. They had roughly two feet of space in between the ridge and the tree branches, but they sat a good foot and a half below the trunk, with just their heads poking up. He managed to sit up, but at an angle, much like a recliner. Thankfully, the thick spread of pine needles, while not the most comfortable, protected them from moisture seeping into their clothes.

Jackie unzipped both backpacks and tilted the bags so the openings were facing them.

"What are you doing?"

"Zippers can be reflective, and we might need something," she whispered back. She grabbed a pair of pants and slid them underneath her like a seat cushion. Another reminder her attire wasn't as equipped for the elements as his.

The wool blanket on top caught his eye. He made quick work with his pocketknife and cut two wide strips. "Wrap around your face and hair. Hurry."

The men were yelling. He kept the makeshift scarf off his ears and strained to hear.

"He's armed."

"We might've hit him."

"I'm not walking in there and making it easy for him to shoot me if we didn't. Is the girl armed, too?"

Jackie reached for his hand as if silently asking if he'd heard the danger nearby. He squeezed in response. Right now they needed to stay utterly still. The high beam swept across the trees. Jackie closed her eyes and tilted her head ever so slightly so all that faced forward was the gray wool blanket. Besides the added warmth, it hopefully made for good camouflage. A good idea, but Shawn needed to remain upright to see what was coming. He squinted through the thick pine needles. He could see movement, but not clear pictures.

Coyotes sounded in the distance, closer than before. An unbidden shiver ran up his spine, shifting the needles ever so slightly. The animal noises kept him from hearing the rest of what the men said. A flashlight beam shifted their way, reflecting off all the snow and shiny needles surrounding them. He held his breath and squinted but forced his eyes to stay open. The beam moved away.

The crunching of snow retreated and Shawn exhaled. Using slow movements, he carefully unholstered his gun and laid it on his lap for quick access. They may have narrowly avoided being shot, but they'd lost their only shelter. A wind gust shook the trees and dumped snow on top of his wool-covered head as if in response.

"Think they'll be back?"

"I'm sure they will. If they're smart, they'll return in the morning. They might even post men to watch the tree line closest to the road."

"That's not encouraging. Does that mean we should keep moving?"

"No, the risk outweighs the potential benefit. But we need to beat them by getting out of here at first light."

Morning couldn't come fast enough.

SIX

The minutes passed at an excruciating pace until the motors had revved far enough away that she felt it was safe to move. Shawn twisted to look into her eyes. "We should stay here until the sky lightens, and then get moving before they come back for a second look."

Logically, the verdict made sense, but she itched everywhere. The wool kept her face from feeling like an icicle, but she'd never been a fan of scarves over the nose and mouth. "It's your turn to sleep," she said. A quick glance at her phone showed the time as just past two in the morning. "I got several hours and I'm wide-awake."

He frowned and she geared up for an argument, but instead he handed her the Taser. "Wake me up if you see anybody." He leaned against the mound of dirt and closed his eyes. He probably wouldn't be able to sleep, as the rocky headrest had to be the most uncomfortable surface that—

His deep breathing fell into a pattern, instantly proving her wrong. Shawn had stayed awake for almost five hours with the silence and cold as his only companion. She didn't know how he'd done it without falling asleep himself.

She gingerly stuck her hand into the open backpack, taking care to be quiet but hoping to find something that would help them reach civilization fast or at least keep her awake. She trusted Shawn would be able to lead them to the archaeologist's trailer. Eventually. But she also knew the painstaking work of mountaineering. It wasn't an exact science.

She slid her hands underneath the backpack's contents and then into each pocket of the pack. Her fingernails brushed against something that crinkled. She cupped her hand around the flashlight on her phone so the beam wouldn't be strong enough to wake Shawn or be spotted outside of the trees. The paper seemed to be a brochure of some sort.

Carefully she unfolded the crude map onto her lap. Even with map-reading skills, she had a hard time making sense of what looked like a homemade document. Most of the map had been colored yellow, with a few black lines curving back and forth and across the paper. Those, she assumed, were roads. No elevations, peaks or legends could be found, not even on the backside. There was a rectangle in the middle with the word *Avoid* written inside it.

Above the warning was a hand-drawn pond—or maybe a lake, since she had no reference for scale. Trees surrounded it. Above the stick-figured trees, a green section filled the rest of the map. A crooked drawing of a square and triangle, vaguely resembling a house, had the penned words *New hut*, between yellow and green sections.

The quality of the map led her to believe the detectorist had created it. Perhaps the document was evidence and could help investigators retrace his steps. When her eyes couldn't handle the strain of studying the details in the dim light, she returned the map to the bag.

She rechecked the backpack before zipping it. A sliver of shiny aluminum caught her eye, sticking out of a pocket she hadn't noticed in the dark. Inside, she found a brand of hand warmers she'd never heard of before. Regretfully, she left them where they were. There was no guarantee when they would have warmth again, and they might need them later if the temperatures dipped even more. She shivered at the thought.

Once her phone was put back away, she forced herself not to keep checking the time. The sky gradually lightened. A hoot of an owl nearby caused Shawn to stir.

He pulled his scarf down and groaned. "We survived the night. I guess that's something."

"Two hikers were rescued today." She used her best newscaster voice. "When found, one remarked, 'We survived. I *guess* that's something.'" He didn't return her teasing smile, though. "Sorry, I've been told I'm a morning person."

"You speak in news bites now, huh?" He stretched his arms upward. "That's new. The 'morning person' part I remember. Should serve you well today. The faster we get moving, the faster you get rescued."

Every muscle ached as she turned to climb out of their tight quarters. She pulled down the edge of the scarf ever so slightly. To the east, the night sky had lightened enough that they could see the snow-covered trees with the stars still twinkling from up above.

"First light," she murmured. The half hour before sunrise had always been her favorite when she'd gone camping with her dad. They'd been the two early risers of the group while Eddie and Shawn inevitably slept until roused.

Those had been the best moments in the wild. Experiencing utter stillness and calm—before the birds sang a single note—heightened the beauty and majesty of nature. In turn, she'd always felt closer to God when surrounded by nothing but His creation. Although for the past few years she'd preferred a civilized version of it…like at a zoo or a resort.

Each step in the snow sharpened the fear that the gunmen might appear at any moment. Shawn took the same care in his steps for a minute before attacking the ground with a little more gusto. "If last night was any indication, we should hear them coming."

They struggled to find a pace that wasn't too fast—if they started sweating, their clothes would get damp, a sure recipe for hypothermia—or too slow so they'd never make it to the trailer by nightfall, or worse, before the storm hit.

"I really should've let someone know I was going to the wedding so they'd know to be looking for me."

She imagined her family getting all dressed up in a few short hours, probably taking family photos without her. Twin Falls, as most would assume, was an unlikely place for a reality star to choose as his home base. But her dad had wanted his children to grow up as close to the wilderness as he had, while her mom wanted to live in a city. The compromise resulted in Twin Falls, a growing town surrounded by unique outdoor terrain with beauty on every side.

Her dad may have grown up camping and hiking, but his real love for survival skills had come during his time as an air force helicopter pilot. Wolfe Dutton never recounted stories from those days, not on his television show nor in real life, but her mom had once confided that he'd rescued many people, some who'd got into danger because they didn't know how to rescue themselves.

Jackie supposed that was what drove him to teach others his survival skills. When his show became a sneak hit, he started his own production company, whose first big purchase was a multimillion-dollar used helicopter that sat fifteen people. He could take his entire production crew out to the most remote areas. Too bad he wasn't in the area filming now.

She stayed in Shawn's footprints, directly behind him. They were both out of breath, which would make them sweaty, and their clothes would get damp. "And then you die," her dad would say. Her dad could take the mildest of decisions to prompt a story that ended with "and then you die."

"The trek would go a lot faster if we had snowshoes of some sort." The clouds gathering far in the west, low and thick, seemed ominous. She didn't know how long the weather front would take to reach them, but it seemed in their best interest to hurry.

Shawn kept trudging until he stopped in front of a tree. He pulled down his scarf and a slow smile spread across his mouth. "Doesn't hurt for Bigtooth Maple to be pruned in the winter."

She didn't need an explanation to know his intent. She picked out branches that were roughly three feet long and flopped them on the snow with the edges pointed upward. Shawn glanced at her choices and picked ones similar. "You're good at this," he said.

"Not really. Certainly not as good as my dad."

They worked in silence until they both had groupings of branches tied to the bottom of their boots. This time they were able to continue walking without sinking so much. The strain on her muscles, though, was no small thing.

Shawn opened his mouth and closed it, shaking his head.

"What? What were you going to say?"

"Is that the real reason you stopped wilderness trekking? Because you weren't as good as your dad? No one can expect to be at his level unless they've lived his life. And even he couldn't anticipate every fall or danger around the corner, even with a map."

"Kind of like how you can't control people or their mistakes, even with love on your side?" She didn't wait for a response. The words just tumbled out and her cheeks heated. She didn't want to start a debate. "Forget I said that. Besides, that's not why I stopped."

Her stomach twisted with the discomfort that came from getting too close to a subject that still brought her shame. "I should've seen the signs a cougar was tracking me, though. I should've been prepared." The memories of the pain flared to life, easily encouraged by the strain her muscles had suffered last night. "A broken bone didn't help matters."

"That must have been terrifying, but I'm surprised you never went back to it. Eddie was, too."

"You guys discussed me?" She put her hands on her hips, trying to be playful, but really she wanted to know what they thought of her. Her parents certainly hadn't said much after the incident. Ironically, the biggest decision of her life at the time had warranted the least amount of discussion, like a taboo subject.

"Well, you weren't my girlfriend yet."

She huffed. "So I was fair game to discuss until then?"

"At least until Eddie could tell I was interested in you and made me promise not to date you." He shook his head. "I always felt guilty for going behind his back. I never specifically agreed to his terms, but I never told him I didn't, either."

"*That's* the reason we dated in secret? I thought we agreed Eddie and my parents would just make things weird." She handed him a water bottle from the pack. Even though drinking cold water in the frigid temps was the last thing she wanted to do, they needed to keep from dehydrating.

"Well, there was that, too. But mostly because he didn't want me to date you."

For some reason, the brotherly protection warmed her heart, though it seemed completely out of character for her twin. Sibling rivalry was more their speed.

"I think we're almost there," Shawn said. "The trees thin out and then stop up ahead. The trailer will be in sight, but so will a lot of the rest of the land."

Jackie dared not hope. The hike had seemed to last for hours, but she had no sense of time without a watch or her phone on. They were close, but would they be able to step out of hiding in the trees without becoming targets? Shawn's forehead mirrored her concern, and they both stilled.

Shawn reached for his gun holster, almost out of habit. He bent over and untied the branches from his boots. Jackie followed suit without a word. While the bare-bones snowshoes helped with long walks, they prevented a stealthy approach.

"Do you have the Taser still?" he whispered.

Her eyes widened, and she pulled the weapon out from the pocket of his coat.

He'd forgotten she was wearing his stuff. "Okay, you can put that back. I'm sure you won't need it," he added hastily. "Just keep it handy. Stay behind me."

As they neared the edge of the clearing, a visual confirmed his worst fear. Two ATVs and a couple of snowmobiles were parked right in front of the archaeologist's field trailer. Two sizable men in full winter gear sat with their hands loosely resting on the handlebars, laughing at each other as if they were having the best day. He'd never wanted to write a ticket for motorized vehicles in unauthorized areas so badly in his life. If these men were responsible for the murders, they'd likely done much worse, but he didn't want to make assumptions.

His bones ached from spending the night in the frigid conditions. A generator, a mini-refrigerator, a hot plate and different kinds of tea and cocoa were all inside that trailer. He knew because on days he was too far from the field office to heat up his lunch when he'd brought leftovers, he'd stopped by the trailer and shot the breeze with Pete, who was often logging archaeological finds, usually minor.

Pete didn't have the best reputation for "street smarts," being considered more of an intellectual than a fieldman. Apparently the job market as an archaeologist proved competitive, and Pete, while disappointed with some of the duties of his position—such as checking to see if an outhouse would contaminate an undiscovered site of historic interest—seemed good at his job. He just hoped Pete had made it back home before the men loitering around his trailer caused trouble.

He placed his hand on the grip of his gun. They were so close to warmth and safety. As long as the men weren't armed, he could tell Jackie to stay back, and handle them.

"What's the status of the storm?" A third man stepped out of the trailer, speaking to the other two still seated on the ATVs. He placed the goggles on top of his head. Shawn hesitated. Were these the same men who had shot at them last night?

The smaller man held up his satellite phone. "Stalled longer than expected in the mountains to the west but expected to hit here in the next twenty-four hours. Supposed to dump an estimated two feet of snow with up to thirty-five-mile-an-hour gusts."

The standing man, seemingly in charge, grunted. "Okay, I think we can get done and out of here as long as the archaeologist cooperates."

"I think he can be made to—"

A gust of wind carried away the second man's words.

Shawn's gut grew hot. Whoever these men were, they had taken Pete. He squinted, trying to make out the leader's face. Before he could take mental notes, his gaze caught on the man's belt. A holster.

The other man who'd been speaking also wore a holster. The third guy had a rifle strapped to his back. He couldn't count on the trailer as his means to get Jackie to safety. He stepped back farther into the grouping of trees to reevaluate. If he could just get his hands on a satellite phone...

A twig snapping behind him caught his attention. He spun around to find Jackie, who stood with her gloved hand over her mouth, her eyes as wide as saucers. A stick sat underneath her boot. She pulled her hand down, mouthing *sorry.*

"What was that?" a man's voice said.

Time to move. Except Jackie bent over with the broken fir branch and rapidly wiped his footprint away. That might have worked last night, but it wouldn't help a bit if the men discovered them standing there.

He went to grab her hand, but she brushed it away and gestured for him to move. He hustled around the largest pine tree closest to them, one that had to be over a hundred years old, judging by its width. Jackie brushed their footprints away until she stood next to him.

He pressed his mouth against her hair. "They'll find us here in a second," he whispered. She pointed underneath the tree.

He almost groaned aloud but didn't have any better ideas. If they ran, the footprints would be a dead giveaway. They both dropped to the ground facing each other, as if about to start doing push-ups, with only an inch or so between their foreheads. He saw the question in her eyes and nodded. They rolled at the same time, until they were underneath the tree branches. Jackie reached out from the prickly cover to brush away their footprints with the same branch she'd used earlier, but her backpack caught on the branch they were hiding under. And judging by the crunch of footsteps, some-one fast approached.

Shawn grabbed the branch from her hand. His back-pack also caught, but he strained, his arms longer than hers, and jiggled the snow until it covered up the foot-prints. Before, the fresh, powdery snow had worked against them, but now he was thankful for how loose and fluid the flakes moved.

"I thought I heard something," a voice announced.

Jackie laid her head on her forearms. As the pine needles were sticking directly into his scalp like an acu-puncture treatment deserving of a malpractice charge, he tried to do the same. The snow below him worked through the layers of insulation in the coat and caused his muscles to tense against the cold.

"I don't see any footprints."

"So animals rustling inside, then. We probably woke up some squirrel from nap time."

"Squirrels don't hibernate."

Shawn's ear was so close to the ground he could hear their boots making a swoosh sound with each step.

"They sleep a lot in winter," the other man re-sponded.

"That's exactly the same thing as hibernating. Nobody there," the voice that'd given the weather report announced.

"It's absolutely not the same thing," the third man groused.

A gunshot rang out and hit the tree next to them.

They both flinched, but somehow kept quiet.

"A little warning next time," one of the men shouted.

"Just making sure you didn't miss something."

"Now they know where we are."

"Good. We've put them on the defensive and they'll get on the move." The older man who seemed to be calling the shots had no shortage of confidence. "They can't hide within those trees forever. If they want to escape the blizzard, they've got to come out into the open. I'll take a spin around the perimeter and make sure you didn't miss tracks. Carl, you take the other side. Spencer, you stay here with Mr. Wooledge. Make sure he stays on task. The clock is ticking."

Shawn felt fingers touch his hand. He fought to look up and found Jackie's hand wrapped around his. She could only lift her head a few inches, as well, but it was enough to read the concern in her eyes. The trailer was no longer an option and the men were hunting them. They were fast losing their chance at survival.

SEVEN

The man was right. They couldn't hide in the trees forever. Evergreens of all sorts made good Christmas trees, but they were not in any way, shape or form good for a deadly game of hide-and-seek.

"Let me make sure that Spencer guy went inside the trailer," Shawn whispered.

His movements made the branches above her wiggle and dump copious amounts of snow on the back of her head. She deserved it, though. She'd been the one who stepped on and snapped the branch. It was just like the incident with the cougars all over again. She should've checked her surroundings—

"Jackie," Shawn whispered. "Come on. I know where we have to go."

He reached a hand out, and as soon as she gripped his palm, he tugged, dragging her out, past whatever had snagged her pack.

Shawn touched his finger to his chest, indicating she should follow him. They moved slower than before. They hiked up a steep incline, only partially obscured from view. The trees thinned in number. Each step was a test of will, as her legs had already been pushed past normal endurance levels.

Jackie found a foothold on a snow-covered boulder. She put her weight on her right foot and the rock shifted. She cried out as she slipped. Strong hands grabbed her waist, lifted and pulled her backward.

"I've got you," Shawn said.

"I'm sorry I yelled. Do you think they heard me?"

A quick look over his shoulder didn't reveal the men, but their motors could be heard in the distance. "Let's hope not." The sporadic wind gusts played with her hearing, and she was no longer sure in which direction the ATVs and snowmobiles were headed.

He tapped the broken rock. "Looks like sandstone to me. Breaks off easily. This hillside is full of it."

"Great. It's going to be slow going, isn't it?"

"Time is not on our side." Shawn reached for her hand. "Let's work together."

Holding his hand felt more natural, though they were both wearing gloves. Trying to escape people who wanted to end their lives left no room for awkward moments.

Almost in tandem, one of them climbed up a few paces, testing the footholds, and then the other caught up using the proven footsteps. They repeated the routine until it felt like they would be taking turns for the rest of their lives.

Shawn hesitated for a second. The small break in momentum gave her a chance to catch her breath. At least he'd chosen a route a snowmobile couldn't mimic. She chanced a glance over her shoulder and spotted the top of the trailer. "We've gone quite a distance," she said. "Too bad we can't keep an eye on those ATVs."

"They're probably checking the roads closest to Darrell's truck. They're assuming we would head for the most common route to civilization."

"Aren't we?" Her voice shook with exhaustion. Without the tough physical task of climbing that took all her mental and emotional energy, she felt at risk of falling apart.

He glanced down at her with one eyebrow raised. "Eventually. Our route is just a little riskier to avoid their perimeter searches. Do you have the Taser?"

She nodded. "I don't have a holster, though."

"It's safe enough to carry in your pocket. The pockets in that coat can zip if you're worried about it falling out. You know how to use it, right?"

"I think so. I took some self-defense classes a few years back." As a single woman living on her own, she'd made it a priority when she was in broadcast news. For some reason, it didn't seem as important now when only her byline showed up in print. "It works the same as the ones available to private citizens, right?"

"The ones on the market incapacitate for a full thirty seconds so you can drop the Taser and run away— better still, drive away. The range is about fifteen feet for personal use, while police-issued ones travel twice that."

"So how long do the ones rangers carry incapacitate? Double the amount, like a minute?" The thought of accidentally setting it off terrified her even more.

"Uh, no. Ones designed for law enforcement only last five seconds."

"What? Why so little?"

"To avoid using force unless absolutely necessary. If we're close enough for the Taser to reach its mark, that should be all we need to disarm and apprehend the suspect."

"Wow." She laughed. "I guess you're not supposed to run away."

He smirked. "Generally not. Unless you're outnumbered with no backup and want to keep a friend safe." He exhaled. "My favorite part of my job is teaching people about the land and the animals. There is so much to appreciate here that isn't noticed by the average park goer."

An unusual swoosh sound followed by drums of some sort reached her ears. "Shawn?"

He took a few steps to the northwest. Through a sliver of bushes and evergreens, a valley could be seen below. "It's the sage-grouse—those funny little birds I told you about."

The birds gathered next to a grouping of what looked like tumbleweed. One of the birds flashed pointy feathers and strutted. It puffed up its chest and made the most ridiculous sound. Whenever the bird walked, its ring of fur rose to its neck like a puffy white collar. "I can't believe that was a *bird*."

"Quite a courting call," he said with a laugh, waving her forward. Every muscle wanted to stop for a while, but his smile encouraged her to keep going. Shawn pumped his arms to get over a particularly thick portion of snow. "I've often wondered if he knows how silly he looks and sounds, and if the female agrees."

"It takes vulnerability to show how much you care about a person. At least she knows she's wanted."

The grouse stopped their song and the air stilled with uncomfortable silence. She'd said too much. Despite her resolve to let the past go, her tongue had a will of its own, determined to sneak in little jabs of reminders. What they needed was a change of subject. "Am I off base or should we be worried about your archaeologist friend?"

He turned to her, his face pale. "You picked up on that? Pete Wooledge is his name—off the record."

"I could find out his name for myself if I wanted. He's in a public position. We are running for our lives, and frankly, at this point, I think everything that's happening is as much part of my personal story as the Bureau's."

"And that's my fault."

She hesitated, choosing her words carefully. "If you hadn't called in that news tip, someone else probably would have. Maybe someone from the construction crew—the foreman was beyond frustrated—and I still would've ended up here."

"Thanks, but I know better."

"How about this—if we get out of this alive, you can proclaim 'off the record' all you like. For now, can you tell me why we're going this way? Where is this risky route taking us?"

"The only hope of the archaeologist surviving is if we get to a phone and get backup." His hand drifted to his gun. "I think we're dealing with looters."

She felt her eyebrows jump. "What kind of looters?"

"If I had to guess, I would say tribal antiquities.

The Bureau finds new tribal sites every year. It's estimated that there are likely thousands more undiscovered sites on Idaho public lands. It's why we have to be so thorough and involve the archaeologists before we so much as put an outhouse on the land."

"So you think these looters are holding Mr. Wooledge hostage and making him find these tribal sites for them?"

"More likely they've already found one and they're making him catalog or unearth it or something. Looters are the most likely group of people to hold an archaeologist hostage. We have a most-wanted list back at the field office. I didn't recognize those men, but I wouldn't be surprised if they've changed their hair or aged since their pictures were taken. Sometimes they sell what they find for personal gain, but others sell to fund terrorist groups."

"Doesn't it seem unlikely that there are so many sites you haven't found?"

"I'm responsible for millions of acres. Millions, Jackie, with all sorts of topography. On top of it all, the Oregon Trail crossed over here and split off into the California Trail, as well. We don't even know all the places the gold-happy settlers tried their hand at mining, even if technically it wasn't their land. So yes, I think given the history and statistics I've been given, it's very likely."

She surveyed the land with new eyes. Nothing seemed flat, but everything seemed beautiful. What other mysteries did the land hold? "So you're saying you have a plan."

"We can't go back the direction we came if those men are looking for us, so we're going to take a bit of a roundabout and sneak behind the back of the plant."

He pointed southeast. "If I remember right, somewhere past this grouping of foothills, there's a rise that builds up to a plateau. If we can get to that, it curves all the way around to the eastern edge of the construction site. I know that the control building of the plant already had a generator and emergency landline installed."

"But that's where the murder—"

He held up a hand. "I know. But that's why we walk on top of the plateau until we get closer to the cement pads. We'll rappel down and sneak behind the construction site until we get to the control building. It's the best option for us to get help, to keep you safe."

"You're not going to try to get the archaeologist first?"

He stopped and stared right into her eyes. "You're my first priority."

The timbre of his voice and the meaning of his words made her heart race. She averted her gaze and turned to the west. From this vantage point she should be able to see mountains instead of a wall of fog. Or was it the storm front?

The thick clouds above made her think of inversions in the Boise area, where air would get stuck in the mountains and become stagnant. Residents were asked to stop using their wood fireplaces during times like that. Here, it meant she couldn't tell where the sun hovered in the sky. "What's the prevailing wind here?"

"West." He pointed to her right. "Come on. Just a little longer and we'll reach the top."

A bullet rang out through the sky and hit the snow ten feet in front of her. "Shawn!"

"It's a man with a rifle. Keep going!"

She hunched over and kept her gaze on the finish line. Almost there. Then they'd be on the other side, hidden. Until the shooter caught up on his snowmobile, at least. She couldn't focus on the despair growing in her chest. Another bullet kicked snow up to her left. The ground gave way and her foot dropped through the snow.

"Jackie!"

Her entire body plummeted through the snow and greeted nothing but air. A scream tore from her throat as she dropped toward a sharp descent. She flung her arms wide and stuck out her feet, crying out as her backside made contact with the thick snow.

She lifted her left knee and twisted it inward, trying to use her boot as a rudder or a brake. Her right leg remained as straight as she could keep it as she sped down the steep snowbank, topping any speed she'd ever achieved on a pair of skis.

"Hold on," Shawn called out.

To what? She kept her arms wide, tucked her chin to her chest and fought to keep her shoulders off the ground. She'd never wanted to be a human toboggan. If she kept the same trajectory she'd slide right over a flat surface with an upward slant. It was likely a rock covered in snow but might as well have been a skateboard ramp.

She dug her left heel and left shoulder into the snow and veered. But not enough. Once again she hit air, except this time she landed on a hard, flat surface and rolled until she came face-to-face with a wolf.

She dared not break eye contact, but she didn't want to appear like she was challenging the animal, either.

He opened his mouth and bared his teeth. She pushed herself up to her hands and knees. The wolf growled, a sound that sent shivers down her spine.

She felt the impact of Shawn landing somewhere behind her. His grunt confirmed he'd survived. "You and cornices really don't get along," he muttered.

"Not the time," she said through gritted teeth.

She straightened, holding her hands out toward the wolf. If it made any sudden moves, though, she wasn't sure what she'd do. And she really didn't need to be reminded that she was not cut out for this. Once again, she'd made a mistake with no hope of rescue, because right behind the wolf stood an entire pack, glancing up from some sort of animal carcass.

Shawn gasped. She could hardly swallow or take a breath. "I think we've interrupted their dinner." She forced herself to lift her arms, slowly, making herself look as tall as possible. Trying to force her face into a fierce expression wasn't working, though. She'd written an article once on fear having a particular scent that animals could smell. This was the only time she wished that her reporting proved to be garbage.

"I really hope we don't look better than the planned menu."

Shawn's breath came out in heaving puffs that floated away, like clouds, in the breeze. They were on borrowed time before the gunmen caught up. At least they were on flat land for once, and Jackie didn't appear to have any broken bones. He didn't, either, though his lower back was likely to file an official complaint later.

The growl from the wolf six feet in front of Jackie didn't help his heart rate recover. He took a step closer and the growl intensified and caught the interest of another wolf that had been content feasting nearby. He squinted for a closer look. The average wolf pack was made up of six to eight wolves.

He spotted twelve. *Please tell me I accidentally counted twice.*

"We don't have time for this. That gunman might have to go a longer route to get here, but he'll tell the others. They'll catch up." Jackie held her arms up in a threatening manner, but the wolf didn't seem the least bit deterred.

Shawn noticed the tip of a three-foot branch caught up in the laces of Jackie's boots. While not very thick, the stick might help their cause. He bent over slowly, not wanting to give the wolf any reason to pounce. "Don't stare into his eyes," he said firmly. "You'll feel a tugging on your boot. Hold your stance."

"It's hard to look at him without looking into his eyes!" Her voice grew in volume and she shook her arms at the wolf. The wolf took the slightest step backward.

"Good." Shawn wrapped his hand around the branch and took a step beside her while swinging the branch upward. The wolf took another step backward. Unfortunately, two more of his buddies developed an interest.

"Shawn—"

"I know. They're probably just guarding their food."

"Okay. Okay. So we back up slowly, right?" She rose on her tiptoes and waved her arms. "Back off!"

He hollered and waved the stick in front of him in an

arc. "That's it. Yeah, let's back away until they aren't interested, but we can't run or—"

"We die. I know. Let's just hope this time I don't fall off a cliff."

He knew she was recalling her incident with a cougar all those years ago. "I admit you don't have the best record with falling."

"You finally understand why my family used to call me Grace."

At any other time he might've chuckled at the memory. They *had* teased her, but that'd all stopped after she'd gone missing. He'd never told her what it was like for him, waiting until the search team had found her. He'd experienced the same feeling when she'd disappeared in that mound of snow at the top of the hill a moment ago.

Shawn waved the stick in front of him again because he wasn't about to go through the feeling of terror again. "Don't show fear, either, and step behind me." He felt Jackie's fingers grab the back of his coat. She tugged, leading him backward. "That's right," he said. "Good. Let's stay together."

"You keep them back. I'll watch our step," she said.

He let his feet slide backward across the snow some more, still wielding the stick that would easily be treated as a toothpick in the jaws of a wolf. Two of the wolves turned and trotted back to the dinner party. The final wolf, the one that had started the standoff, took the slightest step back but kept his teeth bared.

Their boots crunched over the snow. The topography changed. The snow didn't seem as soft underneath their feet. It also seemed icier.

"I think it's working," Jackie said. "He's losing interest." The wolf took four more steps back, huffed and turned away to follow the other wolves.

Shawn couldn't celebrate, though. He'd made a fatal flaw in situation awareness. Even the flat areas of the Idaho wilderness should've had giant lumps from snow-covered tumbleweed or bumpy areas of terrain. There was only one logical reason to find such smooth topography. He should've noticed by now, but the gunman and the wolves had made the blood pound in his head and had turned off all other senses.

She continued to pull on his pack, shuffling backward. "You're going to think I'm crazy, but I thought I felt something move under my feet. It—"

"Jackie, stop!" Even as he said it, he felt the shift. The cracking reached his ears, but he was too late. Gravity tugged on him, breaking through the ice below. His legs hit the icy water before his brain could react. His arms shot upward, losing his grasp on the stick.

"No!" He felt Jackie tug on his backpack, the pressure pulling his arms backward for a minuscule portion of a second before she lost the fight against gravity. She'd pulled the pack off his back, without him in it. His fingers spread apart, desperate to grasp anything but only able to touch the icy water. He sucked in a giant breath before the water closed over the top of his head.

He kicked his legs, frantic to keep from plummeting deeper, but the lake didn't care. He continued to free-fall before bobbing upward. He reached his hands above his head. *Please let me come right back up to the hole.* His palms slammed against a thick slab that might as well have been rock. His throat tightened with a held-back scream, almost releasing what little oxygen he had left. He thrust his legs in a scissor motion, shoving his fists against the ice.

Unyielding.

I don't want to die yet. Don't leave Jackie alone up there with the wolves and murderers. I'm not ready. Please!

His thoughts and prayers ping-ponged in his brain so fast he couldn't comprehend much.

So cold.

The water was almost light enough to see through. Something brushed against his leg. He flinched, spinning around to see—a fish. And there, more light. And a hand? A hand holding the stick he'd lost. It thrashed frantically in the water, stirring up the current.

His arms wouldn't move as fast as he wanted. He reached out for it. The burning in his lungs intensified. The ache in his ribs, desperate to expand, almost consumed him. His legs wouldn't kick the way he wanted anymore. Still, he reached.

His right hand touched the slippery wood and his fingers wrapped around it, as if on their own volition. He stretched his left hand and tried to do the same as he closed his eyes. Just for a minute. To make the pain go away. He vaguely sensed he was moving until his face hit frigid air. He sucked in a breath.

"Shawn!" Jackie yelled in his face. "Don't give up!"

He blinked, as if coming out of a nightmare, except pain like he'd never experienced—like lightning—rushed through all his muscles. He fought to focus. Jackie lay flat on her stomach, on the ground—no, the ice. She could fall through at any second, as well. Adrenaline surged through his veins.

She grabbed his right hand and pried it off the stick to move it to her back. "Grab on to my pack."

He did as she asked. She pulled the stick from his left hand. "Both hands on my pack, and don't let go," she ordered. In a smooth motion, she twisted slightly away from him. The momentum pulled him up enough to get his elbows on top of the ice, but the resulting cracks couldn't be ignored. Her back arched and she stabbed the ice with the end of the stick. "Don't let go of the pack! Try to climb!"

He reached six inches past his first grasp. The pack had twisted to her side from his tugging. She pulled on the stick and slid farther away. Her grunt and the strain it had to be causing her gave him newfound strength. He would not let her die for him. Coming out of a frozen lake that was threatening to pull him back in proved to be the hardest pull-up he'd ever endured. His chest hit the ice.

Crack.

"Hold on." She clawed at the ice, slithering away, pushing his pack in front of her as she went. The movement proved enough to help him get his knee out. He vaulted off that pivot point and slid fully on top of the ice. Water poured off the top of his head.

The threatening cracks paralyzed all movements. Jackie twisted around. "I'm going ahead of you, army crawl all the way. Spread your legs. Spread your weight."

He did as she said, though he wanted off the ice as fast as possible. His muscles threatened to stop working.

"Come on, come on. Only a little farther. Keep moving. A little farther." Jackie continued talking until she came to a halt. Shawn followed her gaze. The wolves had stopped eating and all stared, as if enjoying the show. The sound of motors grew louder, though.

"We can't think about them yet." She slithered on, making sure he followed.

The moment she reached the snowy bank, she scampered up, reached for the back of his parka and pulled him the rest of the way to solid ground. He collapsed into the snow, panting.

"Listen very closely," Jackie said. "You must do exactly what I say without question." Her voice shook and her eyes were the widest he'd ever seen. "Do you understand? We've only got four minutes left to save your life."

EIGHT

Five minutes until hypothermia set in, and they'd already used up at least a minute if not two or three just getting him out of the water and off the lake. If she didn't get him past the immediate danger point quickly, she'd have no means to stop his death. The thought seemed to shut down all other emotion. A type of autopilot she didn't know existed overtook her.

She dropped the sopping wet backpack she'd pulled off his back into the snow. "Keep moving. Keep the blood flowing. The adrenaline is what's going to save you. Embrace it." She spoke rapidly as she unzipped his pack and pulled out all the contents as fast as she could. The water had yet to seep fully into the heavy canvas of his bag. The wool blanket was still dry, as well as the food and a host of other items. The water had managed to soak through the bottom of the pack, but that was where he'd stored the rappelling rope.

She grabbed the snow pants, a flannel shirt and the ripped wool blanket, balled them all up and shoved them into his hands. "Head for behind those trees. Now! You know what to do." He rushed forward in a stumbling type of run to the grouping of bushes twenty feet away.

She turned to the wolves, only a hundred feet or so away from them. She raised both arms, this time unafraid. "You do not want to mess with me right now." She almost didn't recognize the firm, deep voice as her own. For a split second, the wolves turned their heads left and right, almost appearing like domestic dogs trying to decipher a command. But then they went back to their food like the dangerous hunters they were, and her bravado faltered.

A sob had been stuck at the back of her throat for too long. Almost losing Shawn was too much, but they weren't out of danger yet. She couldn't focus on the hard work ahead. She needed to focus on the strength she had. Her father had taught her that. Focus on the positive.

"Except I'm on empty," she whispered. The confession came out more as a prayer. She pulled her shoulders back and lifted a request for His strength before pushing forward. She forced herself not to run, so as not to tempt the prey drive in the wolves. She did walk fast and purposefully, though, as the sound of engines still echoed in the air.

She stopped short and called past the foliage that Shawn had disappeared beyond. As cruel as it seemed, with no fire available, survival training recommended removing wet clothes and rolling around in fresh snow, in hopes the snowflakes would absorb as much moisture as possible.

"Have you taken off the wet items and rolled in the snow? Have you put on the snow pants and blanket?"

"Y-yes." His teeth chattered so loud she could hear it through the brush. "S-s-so cold."

Her eyes flickered to the hills, as the engine sound grew louder. A snowmobile crested one. The gunman had found a way to the top. She didn't need to see what he was reaching for. She turned to run and a bullet tugged on her backpack. She fell down and pushed with her toe into the closest bush.

She crawled forward. A bullet hit the tree above her and bark sprinkled over her like sharp confetti. She forced herself to keep crawling, to keep moving deeper into the foliage. Where had Shawn gone?

"Are you moving?" The amount of restraint needed to keep from yelling in a life-and-death situation tensed her neck muscles to a painful degree.

Silence was the only response.

The bullets stopped. At least the gunman couldn't see her anymore, but it was only a matter of time before he called for the other men to join him. She hadn't seen an easy route for a snowmobile to safely maneuver to the lake area without a steep drop, like they'd endured, but it wasn't as if she had a map of the area to confirm her suspicions.

"Shawn, I need you to talk to me."

She dived through another set of bushes to find him curled up in a ball, shivering with the wool blanket wrapped around his torso and the snow pants on. Definitely meant for a shorter person, the hem of the pants stopped six inches above his ankle.

She ripped off her own backpack, ignoring the bullet hole at the back corner, and pulled her gloves off. While water-resistant, they certainly didn't qualify as waterproof. She searched inside the pack until she found her very chilled, but dry, socks and the fashion boots she'd been in last night.

She sat on the backside of her pack so she could avoid sitting in the snow and took off the detectorist's boots and wool socks. The wool socks were men's size anyway and should fit Shawn, while her thin black ankle socks from last night probably wouldn't have made it over his heel. She made the switch into her old socks and boots as quickly as she could.

"Good thing these socks are long. Put these on." His movements were too slow in responding, so she shoved the wool socks on for him. "These boots are likely to be tight, but at least they're dry."

He looked up and blinked rapidly, his arms still wrapped around himself, covered in the wool blanket. The blue-and-yellow pattern on the flannel he wore would normally have done good things for his complexion, but gray-tinted skin didn't look good on anyone. He needed to get his blood flowing properly again.

"We have to get you moving." She held out a hand. He grabbed it and she almost flinched at his cold touch. "Please start talking to me. I need to know that you're lucid." She reached back in her pack to see if there was anything else she had that could help. "The hand warmers!" She'd forgotten her discovery early that morning.

She found the pouches and quickly scanned the directions. Air-activated, they had double-sided adhesive to strategically place the warmers in boots, on the backs of shirts and in gloves. The glove option was no longer possible since both of their pairs had suffered from the dunk in the lake. Still, she helped him stick two on his socks and two on the back of his shirt. He wrapped the blanket tighter and stuffed the ends underneath the overall-like straps of the snow pants to hold it in place.

She moved to take her coat off.

"No."

She hesitated at his fierce objection. "We need to get you warmer."

He shook his head. "I have the blanket and now these warming pads. You've already given up decent boots."

"That's not enough to actually increase your core temperature, Shawn. Here, let me take the wool blanket."

"No, I got it damp now. I'll be fine."

She knew well enough not to mess with his steely-eyed gaze. His mind was made up. "But what are we going to do? If we make a fire—"

"It'll be like a beacon."

"At this point, I'm willing to take the risk."

He frowned. "I...I don't know. We should at least get farther away from the wolves and gunmen before we decide. The last thing I want is to narrowly avoid death, fall asleep by the fire and wake up surrounded by fangs and guns."

"Agreed." She peeked out of the brush. The snowmobile was no longer visible, but maybe he'd found a path down to the lake. Once again, something triggered her mind. East of the lake, a tall giant rocky plateau rose up in the distance. That had to be the plateau

Shawn said would help them sneak back to the geo-thermal plant site.

The gray clouds hovered so low she couldn't see how far north the tabletop rock extended, though. Some foothills bumped right up against the plateau while another set wrapped around the south end of the lake. They loomed above them like guardians, but south of the hills was a majestic pine forest.

The pieces of their location clicked in place. She was staring at the same locations highlighted on the homemade map. The rectangle must have been the archaeologist's trailer, which meant…

She pointed southeast. Her hand still stung from sinking her fingers into the icy waters. "Shawn, is there a warming hut on top of that foothill?" The hope in her voice almost physically hurt. The desperation to be right was so strong she was terrified of disappointment.

His brow furrowed. "That's USFS land. I think so?"

USFS had to be the Unites States Forest Service. That also confirmed her suspicion. The yellow section of the homemade map was likely Bureau of Land Management property, probably to match the color of their shirts and logo, and the green section would match the Forest Service.

"That's a tough hike," he said, his teeth chattering. "But getting indoors sounds amazing."

She handed him a beef jerky. His fingers were like ice cubes. He may have dry clothes on now, but he wasn't out of the danger zone of hypothermia. They needed to get his body temperature up within the next fifteen minutes, which meant she'd drag him up that hill if necessary. "Eat. Let's keep moving."

He blinked, appearing slightly disoriented. Oh, that was a bad sign. *Please help us make it in time.*

Shawn had never lost control of his body before. Maybe that wasn't what was happening, but his arms and legs vibrated at such an intense rate, far beyond any type of shivering he'd ever endured, that he fought to stay calm. Jackie's deepening frown every time she looked back at him didn't help matters. Maybe he looked even worse than he felt.

She dropped his hand. "That's it." A second later she'd tied one end of his rappelling rope around his waist and one around her own. "As much as I'd like to, I can't throw you over my shoulder and hike up this hill. I need to pump my arms to scale this incline and so do you." She grabbed a handful of chocolate almonds and shoved them in his palms. "Stuff these into your mouth and chew. Your metabolism is through the roof right now in order to keep you warm. Keep eating nonstop."

He did as she asked because it seemed simpler, though he wasn't entirely sure why. Every ranger knew the symptoms of hypothermia. He'd spent many winters educating cross-country skiers about the dangers but never thought he'd fall into the trap. He'd lose street cred if anyone else found out.

"Street cred?" Jackie's voice rose.

He hadn't realized he'd spoken aloud.

"Mental confusion is stage two…or three," she said. "I can't remember, but it's not good." She ripped off her coat. "Don't refuse me now." She forced his arms into the sleeves. She took a wool scarf and wrapped it around his head. That wasn't comfortable at all, as the icicles in his hair pressed against his forehead. She put a hand on each side of his face. "Stay with me."

The rope around his waist tugged him forward. She was ahead of him. He grabbed it with both hands and found he really wanted to follow but kept forgetting why.

Wind whipped her hair, clouding her vision. The intensity didn't seem to show any signs of stopping, either. Her heart pounded so hard she thought it would jump out of her chest. The clouds opened and snowflakes as big as quarters drifted onto her head. Any thicker, and she'd lose her way. The prevailing wind came from the west, Shawn had said, which meant she was still heading in a southeastern direction, unless the wind shifted and she got them lost.

The incline eased and she almost shouted for joy. Her heart raced from the exertion and the heavy breathing hurt. She almost walked into a posted sign against a wire fence that read Don't Walk. Baby Forest Growing Here. USFS.

A hundred feet in front of her was a crescent-shaped snow-covered space with the smallest tips of evergreen trees poking up out of its white blanket. Surrounding the space were magnificent trees that could easily compete for the honor of being lit at Rockefeller Plaza. And to the east, nestled into the front line of trees, was the shape of a wooden cabin.

She cried out. A burst of adrenaline pushed her to

grab Shawn's hand. Her gentle prodding to jog for the building didn't work. He shuffled in the snow, his eyes half-closed, whether from confusion or from his muscles refusing to loosen up enough to run, she didn't know.

So close. They couldn't come so close only to die.

NINE

Shawn woke up in a sweat. He ached everywhere and felt a giant weight on his chest. He blinked slowly. The dim lighting made it hard to identify his surroundings, but he was dry and warm, and staring at a wooden ceiling. Something shifted next to his legs.

"You're awake." Jackie sat propped upright, her back up against a wall, underneath a massive set of windows. From his vantage point, prostrate on the floor, he spotted blankets of vertical fog—likely snow—coming down on the mountain peaks in the distance. The sky looked precariously close to darkness.

"This place faces west, so we can keep an eye on what's going on," she said. "Unfortunately, you can't see as far as the geothermal plant. I think we need to get to that plateau you were talking about to get a good look." She put down what looked like a pamphlet, shifted and moved to her knees. She placed a warm palm on his forehead. "Your fever broke."

She stood and moved to the smallest stove he'd ever seen, where she picked up a cast-iron kettle and poured liquid from it into a metal cup. "The Bureau really needs to reach out to the college students that built this warming hut so they can build more of them in the area. I've been reading about it while you slept. They built this as an experiment to see if a solar heating pump would work for a warming hut for snowmobilers. Then the trail society put in a propane stove as an added bonus." She crossed the room and set down the cup. "Do you think you can sit up?"

He yawned. The smells of pine and cedar and faint remnants of the fire ashes filled the room. He replayed everything she'd just said when he was barely awake. "Yeah." His voice sounded more like a frog croaking.

She tried to reach for his arm to pull him up, but he didn't need the help. He had a headache, his muscles felt a little sore and his skin a little tingly, but other than that, he seemed back to normal. "I can't believe it's actually toasty in here."

She cringed. "I'm afraid we might be running out of heat soon. I cranked the radiator to the max setting. The brochure says six hours of use with the solar pump." She pushed the warm mug into his hand. "Drink. Warm liquids will make me feel better about your core temperature."

The water was, in a word, disgusting. The metallic taste didn't help his mood, but the rest of his body seemed to appreciate it. The next few minutes he endured her orders to eat and drink more until his mind finally cleared enough to engage.

"I'm fine, Jackie." He reached for her hand, then looked out the window and groaned. "Any sign of the gunmen? What time is it?"

She shook her head and powered up her phone. "Still no signal, by the way. It's just after four o'clock."

He groaned again. "That means we only have an hour before sunset. We've been here for *hours*."

"I know, but your safety was more important to me, and I wasn't sure what to do. Leaving the heater behind is going to be hard to do." She gestured to the side door. "Do you know they also have a bathroom? Compost toilets." Her eyes twinkled. "You really have got to get the Bureau to upgrade—"

"The Bureau manages more land than the Forest Service, but *they* get a bigger budget and three times as many employees." He held up a hand. "Not that it's a competition."

She grinned. "Ah, so I've touched on a sore subject."

"The sore subject is what we do next." He picked up the pamphlet she'd left on the floor. "We need to get to that control room that has a phone, and call for help."

Jackie lifted her chin to look out the window. "The wind isn't messing around, Shawn, and I don't like how that storm front looks."

He followed her gaze. The blizzard was fast approaching. "Exactly my point."

"But there's a woodstove here. If the blizzard hits before we make it to the building, we're talking white-out conditions for those looters out there, as well as us. If we stay here, we might be able to risk a fire. They wouldn't be able to see it." She crossed the room and pointed to a door. "There's a changing room that would be big enough for me to sleep in so we could each have privacy."

He wasn't sure how to tell her...

Her expression clouded as he finally met her gaze. "We can't stay here, though, can we?" she asked. "The archaeologist."

He nodded, relieved she understood. "Besides, if those men know the land like they seem to, they'll eventually find their way here. I know I haven't been much help today, and my first priority is to get you safe. But I also can't ignore the fact that those men have Pete and might leave him to die in the blizzard."

Even more likely, the men might murder Pete when they no longer needed him, but Shawn couldn't bear to voice that possibility.

"I understand." She placed a hand on top of his and her cheeks flushed. "You feel warm again. That's good." She stared hard for a few seconds before her shoulders sagged. "I was so scared you were getting close to the dangerous zone. I couldn't remember all the stages of hypothermia."

"Your quick thinking and—" he reached down to pull off the itchy warming pads still in the boots "—ingenuity in what I could do to get warm made all the difference." He frowned as he noticed an extra coat on top of him with the USFS logo.

"I figured out how to open the ranger's closet. There wasn't much except that mug, some cleaning supplies and an extra USFS uniform, including the coat. I figured rangers are—at least philosophically—coworkers in a sense and wouldn't mind. I just piled it all on top of you in lieu of blankets."

He took the pile of clothes she handed him and stepped into the restroom for a moment to change. While it seemed like a small act of betrayal to wear the green forestry uniform instead of his normal tan, he'd never been so thankful for dry, warm clothes. He opened the door to find her at the propane stove.

"You saved me," he said. "Thank you." He noticed the two folding chairs pulled up close to the radiator with his clothes hanging on them, drying. She'd stayed busy while he'd slept.

"Well, it's my fault you needed saving."

He folded his arms across his chest. "Maybe my mind is a little fuzzy, but I don't follow. How do you figure?"

"Like you said, I really don't get along with cliffs."

He felt his eyebrows jump. "You don't really think you could've avoided that fall through the snow today, do you? Even the great Wolfe Dutton—no pun intended—wouldn't have been able to avoid the wolves, especially with someone shooting at him. Is that his real first name? Because I don't think I questioned it growing up." He had to stop for a second. What other thoughts did he need to revisit from his childhood? "And, even then, Wolfe experienced his share of falls—"

"Only dramatized falls. The time he fell through a cornice, he'd already canvassed the area with his crew and knew it'd be a safe drop. And no, his real name is Walter, but that doesn't sound nearly as adventurous as Wolfe, does it?" She shivered. "Although I'm not as fond of the name after coming face-to-face with wolves."

How could she really think today was her fault? He studied her face and the lines around her eyes. "Are you really still affected by that night all those years ago? When you were stuck on that ledge," he added. "That night was more traumatic than we all imagined, wasn't it?" His last question came out in a gentle whisper.

He averted his gaze the moment he asked. He hadn't meant to get so personal or sound so caring. Maybe he could blame his sudden emotional weakness on the lasting effects of hypothermia, but he'd be fooling himself. The more time he spent with her, the more he wanted to be with her. The tenderness in her eyes had been knocking down all the guarded areas of his heart and leaving him vulnerable yet again.

The atmosphere in the room seemed to shift at his unexpected question. "It doesn't occupy my mind all the time," she finally said. "But I also can't seem to get away from my dad's reputation, so I constantly feel pulled back. My first real job was as a reporter for the local news station. It was the same station you called."

He shook his head. "I didn't know that."

She shrugged. "The job was a short-lived stop in my career. I told everyone that the sensationalist nature of television didn't appeal, but that was only half the story." The tension in her ribs started to dissipate as she spoke. "The news director wanted to have a weekly feature where I would attempt survival stunts."

His eyes widened. "Wow. I take it you refused?"

"Until it became an ultimatum. They felt certain, given my relationship to the great Wolfe Dutton, that it would boost ratings—even if I failed horribly, which I knew I would."

"Probably even more viewers if you failed."

She laughed at the thought. "You might be right, but I moved to reporting for the paper instead. I figured if they couldn't see my face, then they wouldn't be tempted to make it an issue."

"But you still get assigned the stories in the wild."

"With a lot of encouragement to reminisce about my childhood and experiences with Wolfe Dutton. I *did* have a lot of wonderful adventures as a child, but they're my stories, and I don't know if I want to share, especially not for my job." She sighed. "I look forward to writing a feature big enough that I can call the shots on the stories I'd like to write without having to go as far as changing my name."

"So the hardest part of trying to say goodbye to the wilderness has been your job?" His question had a joking lilt to it, but something raw stirred within her, maybe because of lack of sleep.

She moved to help him finish packing up the gear. If she kept busy, she wouldn't seem as vulnerable. Shawn handed her one of the makeshift scarves she'd placed near the heater to dry. She wrapped it around her neck. "When I was little, it was all about proving I was just as good as Eddie. But I never loved the adrenaline of conquering the wilderness like my dad did."

"I suppose that's natural when you have a twin brother."

"Maybe, but when I gave it up, I felt a little like I gave up the one thing my dad and I had in common."

Shawn chuckled, shaking his head.

She crossed her arms across her chest. "Why is *that* funny?"

"Because you and your dad are two peas in a pod." He held out his hand and tapped his index finger. "I've never met two people so determined to achieve their goals." He tapped his second finger. "You're both the most passionate people on the planet." He tapped his third finger. "Fierce and full of grit with the most out-of-the-box ideas to make things happen—"

"Even if you're right, I'd still like to reach my dreams on my own merit."

"No one really is self-made, Jackie. Maybe if you embraced who you are and stopped worrying about trying not to be like your dad, then you'd have already written the features you wanted."

She bristled at the notion that he understood her job better than she did. The topic had turned the focus too much on her, but the moment of vulnerability poked at her heart, tempting her to say the thing that had been flittering in the recesses of her mind all day.

He sighed at her silence. "I probably spoke out of turn. We need to hurry," he said. "The sun and our reprieve from the weather are disappearing."

The temptation grew to bursting. "Before we walk out that door together, can we set the record straight so I can move on?"

Apprehension lined his face. "Okay?"

"That's more of a question than an answer, but I'll take it. You said that we would've never worked out. I understand why we wouldn't *now*, but why back then? We had a plan to go to school together. No more secret dating after Eddie left for the army…" She held her hands out, unsure whether she really wanted the answer or not.

He dropped his head and shoulders. She almost didn't recognize the suddenly defeated man in front of her. "You probably won't understand, but I knew I'd never be good enough for you or your family. Probably not for anyone. It's that simple."

That was the last thing she'd ever expected. "My family isn't perfect. I'm not perfect. I think you already know that, though. This is about the night of Eddie's accident."

He crossed the room to put away the mug. "The whole unconditional love thing is either a myth that some people are too stubborn to admit, or it's real but only for people who grow up with it."

She crossed her arms over her chest. "What if it's neither? I'm pretty sure God's the only one truly capable of perfect love. We can decide to love like that, but we're sure to royally mess up along the way."

He pointed at her. "See? That's just what I'm getting at. The messing up is what hurts people. This way, whatever I do only affects me."

"You can't believe that. Even if you live in the middle of nowhere, give me a week to investigate and I guarantee I can prove your choices still impact others."

He studied her for a full ten seconds before the intensity of emotion seemed to magnify in his face, as if he'd just solved a problem. "Is that why you became a journalist? To investigate how choices impact others?"

Every time she started to think that he didn't know her very well anymore, he pulled some profound observation out of his hat. It infuriated her that he was right. "Somewhat." A reflection out of the window caught her eye. "Shawn. Get down!"

She crouched, her fingertips holding the windowsill. She lifted her chin until she could peek over the edge. "I saw light reflecting off the snow below." She pointed. "There's the beam again. Some ATVs are on a corridor of some sort between the foothills."

He groaned. "They doubled back, then. I knew they'd check this route. That's the way the construction workers take to get back to town. The path avoids the lake."

"Why didn't we take that?" The thought that they needlessly suffered through an interchange with wolves and a frozen lake was almost too much to bear.

"Because to get on that path, you have to be to the east of that field trailer, out in the open. We would've been seen. I kept us on the most covered route to avoid being discovered."

She grabbed the binoculars out of the pack and focused on the ATVs. After three tries with the dials she finally got the focus right. "I can't see their faces, but they sure look like a couple of the same men." She let out a long breath of pent-up frustration. "Where does the route go?"

He paled. "It will lead them straight here."

TEN

The lights bounced up and down like a roller-coaster ride. Shawn accepted the pair of binoculars from Jackie. "I'd guess they're half a mile away." A snow-plow appeared to be attached to the nose of the first ATV. The second vehicle stayed close, dragging a small trailer, like the type that would usually transport such a vehicle.

"Do you think they've got the stuff they've been looting in that trailer?" Her fingers gripped the window ledge. "You don't see the archaeologist on either of the vehicles, do you?"

He took another look. "I only see two men on the ATVs, but it's possible they're carrying antiquities. If so, they might not need Pete anymore." He pressed his lips tight together. If they hurt him…

"You think they are coming straight for us?"

Shawn lowered the binoculars and frowned. "Since they're carrying a trailer, we can hope they aren't hunting for us."

Jackie shivered. "Unless they plan to kill us, put

us in the trailer and stage an accident like that Darrell guy."

He raised an eyebrow. He hadn't considered a person being in there. What if Pete was trapped in there? "Most likely they're headed for the closest town. Due east. They'll take a sharp turn and head away from us on the snowmobile paths." If only voicing his hopes aloud made them come true.

"If we're that close to a town now, can we follow them at a distance?" She wrapped her arms around herself. "I've never missed central heating so much. Oh, and a real meal, not trail mix or jerky." Her stomach gurgled loudly.

He blew out a long breath and tried to ignore the way his own stomach churned. "If only. On a snowmobile or ATV it'll take them half an hour—maybe longer at their current speed—to get there. It would take us twenty times as long on foot with constant steep inclines and declines to hike."

She exhaled. "Judging by the clouds to the west, the blizzard is almost here."

"We definitely wouldn't make it to town before we were trapped. In whiteout conditions, I don't know that area well enough to lead us." He gestured with his head to the north. "I think we have a better chance of getting on that ridge and sticking to plan A."

He handed her the binoculars so she could see for herself. "Notice how it's at a diagonal? We would travel more as the crow flies, and it's all downhill. I'd guess we'd only have a mile on it until we'd reach the lowest point where we could rappel down. From there, we'd just need to sneak to the back edge of the plant.

That might take us another hour, but then we'd be to the control building with a phone and a generator to run the heat."

"So we have a plan, but that doesn't account for the fact that those men are heading straight here, right now." Her voice rose and wobbled as she returned the binoculars to him.

He accepted and reached for her hand. "Don't worry. There's no need to stop here. They'll make a slight left and be on their way without so much as—"

The ATV with the plow rounded the top edge, now level with their location. The headlights bounced over a bump and swung to the right, directly into the warming hut window. Right at them.

"Duck!" they both said at the same time.

She grabbed his backpack and slid it in his direction, across the slick floor. She zipped up her coat and threw on her pack in a heartbeat. The design of the warming hut didn't leave much in the way of hiding spots. The ranger closet might be a possibility, or the bathroom with compostable toilet, but if the men checked either one, they would be trapped without an exit. The hut had been built with fire escape in mind, though, so there was a back door. Unfortunately, the back wall was practically made up of windows, as well. There was nowhere decent to hide.

The other ATV motor approached and quieted. One of the men shouted in the distance, his words muffled by a gust of wind that howled against the door. Footsteps crunched against the snow.

"Back door," Shawn whispered. They ran across the floor together and burst into the cold. He cringed at the sudden change in temperature, remembering all too well the level of cold he'd experienced hours ago. He never wanted to go swimming again.

Jackie raced ahead to a spot without windows and pressed her back against the thick wooden siding. Shawn mimicked her actions a half second later. The shadows worked to their advantage, covering the side of the building in darkness. A man shouted something about the heat and the oven still being hot. He looked upward. Couldn't one thing go right today?

"It's time to give it up," another man yelled. "I saw you fall into the lake. It's time to show yourself if you want to live."

"They know we're here," Jackie whispered. "One look out the back window, and they'll see our footprints."

Shawn searched the area for a solution. They couldn't outrun the men, especially if they returned to their vehicles. His muscles felt like they'd just endured a marathon after the ice incident. He had replaced his holster, so he had his gun, but there were at least two armed men out there. He slipped the gun from his belt.

Jackie stared at his hand with questions in her eyes.

He couldn't shoot to kill without risking Pete's location dying with them. He needed to arrest them, get to a phone and call for backup and a search party. "If we can separate them, I can disarm them, one at a time."

The moon highlighted the closest tree, a giant oak that didn't so much as budge with the wind, towering above them. Without leaves, the branches wouldn't offer them any camouflage, but the close proximity to the roof would allow him to gain a good vantage point and be able to use the element of surprise. Rarely did people look up.

He pointed to the tree. "Climb." If ever there were a degree for climbing trees, Jackie would've earned it by the time she was in third grade. So he had no reservations that she could still do it.

She nodded. "Lead the way."

He almost argued, but he was slower than her. Strategically, he grabbed at the lowest hanging branch and vaulted up the tree. Years of practice meant he didn't need to study physics to know how to scale the oak using the least amount of energy and strength possible. His feet took much of the weight, but his body had taken a beating over the last couple of days, so every movement hurt. He glanced down to see if Jackie was right behind him.

She wasn't there. His stomach flipped. He searched frantically, poking his head on either side of the trunk, looking for her. Footprints reflected off what little light still shone from the sky. He spotted her at the edge of the grouping of evergreens. His heart raced. It took all his self-control not to yell, "What are you doing?"

Two bullets rang out into the night sky. "I'm losing my patience," a man hollered. "We're going to catch you sooner or later. The faster you show yourself, the faster we can all get warm. Unless you'd prefer to die in the blizzard…"

As if they'd forget about the two murders the men were responsible for and surrender? He'd take their chances with a blizzard any day. He couldn't see the men, not even the one who was doing all the yelling, and he still had no idea where they were. They had to be out front searching for them. Jackie spun around at the tree line and her gaze found him. She held up one finger as if to say "one second," and then she made a second path, heading right back to his tree, but this time walked backward.

Instantly, he understood. She wanted to make a fake set of tracks to make it appear as if they'd run deeper into the forest. A diversion would give them time to escape, maybe even commandeer their vehicles and go straight for town. A smart idea, if only they had more time. Any second—

One of the men rounded the east side of the building. Shawn froze, paralyzed at the thought of what was about to happen. The man pulled out a handgun and aimed it at Jackie. She didn't see him, though. She was too busy keeping a lookout on the opposite side of the building.

Shawn kept one hand on the tree trunk, aimed and yelled, "Drop your weapon!" The man spun in his direction, gun still in hand. Shawn fired and the man dived to the ground.

A bullet whizzed past Shawn's ear from the opposite direction. He twisted to see the second man below, aiming a gun directly at him. A rustling of tree limbs in the distance caught their attention.

"Go after her," the second man yelled to the first. "She's getting away!"

Shawn used the distraction to make his move. He lunged for the roof, except his backpack caught on something. He struggled against the branch's pull on the pack, as the first man took off after Jackie. Shawn slid out of the handles.

The second man moved his aim back to Shawn. "What goes up must come down," he said with a sneer.

Shawn grabbed the dislodged pack and threw it. The pack met its mark, hitting the gunman's nose. Shawn leaped from the thick branch to the roof, no longer worried about stealth. He needed to get to Jackie before the other gunman did.

He landed and dropped into a crouch, doing his best to sink his feet and fingers through the snow to find a grip on the roof. Not much stuck to the metal shingles, but it proved slicker than he would've liked. He scampered up one side and slid down the opposite side of the roof. Without a gutter to stop his descent, he slammed into the ground, dangerously close to the ATV plow, in the giant mound of snow the blade had pushed aside. He rolled off and climbed up the side of the ATV. The keys weren't left in the ignition.

His hamstrings stung from the effort of jumping to standing, but he pushed through the pain and launched into a sprint, banging on the trailer as he passed. Jackie's imagination got the best of him and he feared she might be right about the trailer being used as hostage storage. Not a single noise, though. Unless Pete was already dead. Shawn shook off the thought and darted into the first grouping of evergreen trees. Jackie was somewhere within them, along with the other gunman.

He lifted up a silent prayer that he'd be the one to find her first.

Jackie's heavy breathing would give her away, she was sure of it. She couldn't run in the deep snow, her feet crunching with every step, without being found instantly. The grouping of evergreens, taller than the likes she'd normally seen, discouraged passage. The sunset gave way to darkness in the forest. The branches, heavy with snow, hung down like giant fingers eager to grab her.

The snow had come down harder here—or, more likely, the sun's rays didn't quite make it through the thick vegetation to melt the snow as easily. The heavy buildup underneath the trees meant there'd be no hiding places.

The crunching of footsteps behind her grew closer, faster. An unleashed scream continued to build, tightening her chest and neck, until she wasn't sure how much longer she could hold it inside. She pushed past two tree branches.

The land opened. No more trees. In front of her an expanse covered in dark shadows stretched for at least a mile, lit up only by the moon rising. The sun had completely disappeared behind the mountains to the west.

With every step she took, four crunching footsteps could be heard rushing her way. There was no time to hide her tracks. *Please cover me, Lord.*

Her toe caught a rock and she tripped. Pine needles slapped her face as she fell to her hands and knees, right through the branches. The clouds shifted and the moon shone over the beautiful expanse of rolling hills. Tall grasses poked out of the blanket of snow, and a few monoliths stood guard in the distance. Giant boulders peppered the field and wore stacked snowflakes like Santa hats.

Not a single tree to be found on the lot in front

of her, though. Nowhere to hide. She would have to run in the deep snow, flat out, for five minutes before she reached one of the towering monoliths. Even then, there was likely nothing behind it besides more open space. She'd be an easy target. And what about Shawn? Had he escaped or was he—

Judging by the footsteps, there was definitely more than one man following her, which could only mean one thing. They weren't after Shawn because they'd already got him. Her eyes burned hot with sudden tears, the moisture leaking slightly and stinging her skin. But she needed to see clearly. Now wasn't the time to lose it.

She blinked rapidly. This was her fault. She kept listening to her gut on instinct, the way she'd been trained, but when was she going to get it through her thick head that she wasn't her father? She had no business trying to help. She should've just gone up the tree instead of trying to fool the men into following her fake tracks.

The sound of other footsteps stopped. Her ears strained. Whispers filtered through the branches. "You go that way. I'll take this side."

They were going to ambush her, then. They had guns. She had nothing but a Taser she'd foolishly stuffed in the backpack with everything else, in too big of a hurry to be more strategic.

If Shawn had managed to stay alive despite the gunshots she'd heard, she needed to keep her wits about her. If they caught her or tried to shoot her, he would come for her. The certainty surprised her. This was different from the night of the accident, the night he'd left.

She'd seen the determination to get her to safety in his eyes ever since he'd rescued her. Whatever messed-up notion he carried about not being good enough, she knew he wouldn't let her die without a fight, which meant he would die trying to save her.

She couldn't allow that. With a new rush of determination, she picked up the rock that had tripped her, bolted upright and sprinted for the boulder fifteen feet away. She kicked her foot out and dropped to the ground, sliding behind the boulder like going for home plate. The moment she squeezed between the tall grass and the boulder, she popped up on one knee and threw the rock at the closest evergreen tree. She hit her mark and snow cascaded down from that tree and another whose branches intertwined it. The snow would cover her tracks.

She dropped down into a seated position and leaned over, her head between her knees. *Please cover me and protect Shawn.* The prayer ran on a loop in her head as the seconds felt like minutes.

She couldn't afford to move in the snow without the men hearing her. She wrapped her arms around her legs and covered her mouth to muffle her heavy breathing and the cloudlike vapor it produced. Her heart pounded hard against her ribs. Her throat stung with the shallow inhalations of freezing air.

Branches rustled. "You see her?"

"No. You?" the deeper voice of the two asked. A light beam traveled over her head to the ground not more than three feet in front of her. She held her breath.

The bushes moved, but not from wind. Something had erupted from its slumber. A squeak escaped her lips as the flock of dozens of birds that took flight covered her mistake.

The beam of light moved upward, illuminating the animals. The funny-looking birds, the sage-grouse, flew low to the ground, their wings fluttering so hard they sounded like a fleet of miniature helicopters taking off.

A bullet shot into the night. The sound of wings continued flapping, drifting off into the distance. Her heart beat against her chest so hard she was sure the men would be able to hear.

"You missed," the deep voice said.

"Warning shot. What were those freaky, bearded chicken things, anyway?"

"I don't know, but you've just given away our location to the ranger."

"He missed me. He's not a good shot."

"What if he didn't mean to hit you? He told you to put your gun down."

"Either way, then, we don't need to worry about him making trouble when we leave."

Hope soared. The ranger they'd mentioned had to be Shawn. So he was alive. But if they weren't worried about him making trouble, what did that mean? The beam of light bounced around the ground again.

Jackie forced herself to raise her head just enough to see over her knees and get a better view of her surroundings. As soon as the men were gone, she'd need to leave her hiding place. No cliffs or drop-offs were apparent from this vantage point, but there were a lot of things to trip over. The areas in front of the monoliths seemed to have less snow, as if they'd been groomed before, almost like snowmobile paths. Odd.

"I'm not going any farther," the scratchy voice concluded. The light clicked off. "You know why. Maybe she doubled back and went into the trees, headed the opposite direction."

"Or you could think of it as your motivation not to get on the boss's bad side and check it out just in case," the deeper voice responded.

"That job wasn't supposed to be part of the deal. I'm not going back there, so drop it. You got the ranger's gear?"

Their conversation didn't make any sense. Where didn't he want to go? What job wasn't part of the deal? She really hoped he meant killing them wasn't part of the deal.

"Yeah, I got it." A zipper being opened sounded closer than Jackie liked. "Water bottles, food, a blanket… He's not going to make it to town before the blizzard. No way they're going to survive without this stuff."

"What about the warming hut?" The crunching of snow followed his question.

"We'll disable it on our way back. Things will be worse for us if we don't stay on schedule."

She relaxed ever so slightly, pulling her coat tighter. If the men took what she'd deduced was the snowmobile path, they would round the bend and see her. She needed to find Shawn and hide. It would take those men a few minutes to weave their way back through the forest to the warming hut. Still, she waited until there was utter silence.

She moved to get up. An owl broke the quiet with

his song. She froze. The owl called out again. Wait. Though it sounded remarkably similar to a real one, if she listened closely, this "owl" was increasingly enunciating his sounds. That was no owl. The call almost sounded like *Who cooks for you?*

Her dad had once taught them that the word choice allowed them to mimic the cadence of an owl call better than a simple repetition of "hoo." They used to play epic games of hide-and-seek in the mountains, teasing each other with the calls. She hesitated. Was her voice strong enough to sound authentic?

She took a breath and tried. Footsteps answered her own high-pitched call, though she slurred her words together more to sound realistic. The trees moved slightly and Shawn stepped out into the moonlight. Her heart almost stopped at the sight of him standing there. She rushed for him. He followed her lead and ran toward her. Without thinking, she opened her arms, and they embraced.

She pressed her cheek on his chest, his coat open enough that she could hear the rapid beating of his heart underneath the forestry uniform. He wrapped his arms around her tightly, pulling her closer. His chin rested on the top of her head. "I was so worried about you," he whispered. "I didn't want to risk shouting your name. I'm thankful you remembered."

She laughed but didn't move away. "Your call was a little too enunciated."

"I was afraid you would think I was a real owl."

"You're not *that* good," she teased.

"It's been a long time, though." His voice softened, as if his words held more meaning.

"Yes." It had been a long time since they'd adventured together, but the embrace brought back sweet memories, as well. A motor revved, giving her confidence they could talk louder. She lifted her head to look in his face. "Did you hear them talking? They're on some sort of schedule, but they'll be back to disable the warming hut."

He dropped his arms. "Let's step into the line of trees." They huddled side by side among the trees as the ATV motor grew louder. Huh. She really thought they would've passed through by now and she could only distinctly hear one. It almost sounded as if they were trying to warm up the engine, maybe because of the frigid temperatures.

"They didn't want to go after me in the open field," she said. "Seemed odd to me."

"They probably didn't know if you were armed or not."

"It almost sounded like they'd been here once, though." She supposed it didn't matter now. "How'd you get away? I heard shots."

He exhaled. "By the skin of my teeth. How'd you?"

"I think God answered my prayer. Maybe that sounds ridiculous, but I was able to hide and the sagegrouse offered a diversion. I think I see why you like those birds."

"Doesn't sound ridiculous to me." He smiled. "I like them even more now. Your dad was the one that helped me appreciate the way the ecosystem was created. I'm not against progress or hunting. I just want to protect the land." Howls filled the night sky and a gust of wind drowned out the noise. "At the moment, I'd be fine if the land had less animals that could eat us."

A shiver ran up her spine.

Shawn put an arm around her shoulders. "Are you okay?"

"I should be asking you that. You barely recovered from the lake. And were they right? Did they get your pack with the supplies?"

"I'm afraid so." He sighed. "All the more reason to start moving. I feel like a hypocrite hiking in the dark when I spend my days preaching against it." He picked up a stick and handed it to her. "You know the dangers, too, but I don't see any way around it."

"Do you know this area?" Jackie asked. They were saying goodbye to their last chance at shelter, so she fought against his impatience to leave if those ATVs would just move on to wherever they were going.

"Enough," he said. "I've groomed a portion of the snowmobile trails nearby. The USFS land juts into our Bureau territory for only this bit. The rest of their land is all south of here. We need to cross north over the trail the ATVs used and we'll be on the plateau. If we stick to the backside of it, closest to the trees there, we will be covered. Then when we get to the narrowest point we can rappel down."

Jackie rifled in her pack. "I have one bottle of water left, a couple snacks and one of your ropes. But that's it." She gasped. "Shawn, my purse is still in my pack! Don't you see? That means I still have my car keys. Even if we can't find a phone, if we get to the control building, my car is there. We should be able to drive away."

For the first time since the nightmare had started, she finally felt like they could do it. They could get to safety.

He grinned. "That'd be great, but let's not get our hopes up. Driving in a blizzard—"

"I have chains in my trunk and a shovel." She shook her head, beaming. "Nothing will be able to stop me."

He raised his eyebrows. "Which tells me you're still a survivalist. You just prefer the urban jungle."

"And you prefer forestry over enforcer?"

He laughed. "Wrong agency, but yeah."

She moved the key to the front zippered pocket of the pack, for quick access, and returned her pack to her back. She was ready to face the storm now that they had a plan *and* a backup plan.

The click of metal sounded and in an instant she knew their plans had been destroyed. "Hands up," the gruff voice said. "No turning around."

She dared to glance at Shawn, only to find his face pale. The man behind him pressed a gun into the back of his coat.

"Face forward," he barked. The sound of static filled the air. "I've got 'em. Right at the tree line. Over."

"Got it. Be right there. Over," the younger voice answered.

The motor instantly died and only the sound of wind whistling through the tops of the trees took its place.

"Seems I owe my partner some money. He had the idea of running the ATV motor nearby so you two would think you were safe enough to find each other. Didn't think the motor would cover up all my footsteps but guess he was right."

The man in question joined them almost instantly, his rifle pointed right at Jackie. He'd been the one to shoot her pack earlier, then.

"They were just talking about the danger of hiking," the gruff voice said. "I think that sounds like a fine idea. Get moving."

She wrapped her fingers around the makeshift walking stick still in her hand and stared into the ever-darkening sky. Did she dare try to use it as a weapon? One little stick couldn't overpower a rifle and a handgun before someone pulled a trigger, though. She dropped her head against the wind and took a step forward, having no idea where they were being led.

Shawn wasn't the only one who warned against the dangers of hiking at night. Her father had drilled the sentiment in her own mind, as well. No matter what happened tonight, she knew without a doubt they were about to face death.

ELEVEN

Shawn zipped up the coat he was wearing as the man shoved him forward with the end of his gun. They seemed to want them to go straight ahead, away from the ATVs and the warming hut.

"I wasn't kidding," the man with the rifle said. "I don't want to go out there again."

"You don't have to do anything but make sure they follow my directions."

They trudged forward. Jackie took a step closer to him and their shoulders bumped. "Sorry," she said. "The gusts are getting stronger."

"Keep moving," the man said.

They quickly discovered the bumpy portion of the terrain, tumbleweed, rocks and bushes hidden underneath the thick layer of snow. Jackie tripped and fell forward, crying out.

Like a punch to the gut, he couldn't stand to see her in pain. Even for a second. He dived for her, but the man grabbed the back of his coat. "Oh, no, you don't. Keep the hands up."

"He still has a weapon," the younger man yelled.

He gestured wildly with the rifle. "Take it out of the holster and kick it."

He pressed the release in his holster. There went the last bit of protection he could offer Jackie. He tossed the weapon to the side then leaned over to help Jackie. His eyelashes filled with flakes a second after he'd blinked them away.

"Are you okay?"

She nodded but didn't attempt to speak. That wasn't good. Jackie only stayed quiet when she was really upset or hurting. He wanted to pull her into a hug again. The way she'd reached out to him earlier...

The surge of feelings took him by surprise and left his throat and gut feeling hot and tense. She reached for his hand and he pulled her up to standing as the men started yelling for them to hurry up.

He adjusted his stride to match hers so she wouldn't fall again without his arms there to catch her. Very few thoughts crossed his mind, since the work of hiking in the storm took great concentration, but their recent conversations replayed in his head. Even if he did get a do-over from that night he'd left, if he had a chance to properly say goodbye before they parted ways, he had a sinking feeling this time it would be much harder to let her go.

Still, she remained utterly quiet. Maybe she'd been injured and didn't want to tell him. Like the splinters from earlier, she'd rather keep her mouth tight than complain of pain. Her competitive streak could be exasperating at times, but it served her well when grit and endurance were required. She'd never leave him without a fight. The thought took him by surprise, and with a jolt he also realized the gun wasn't pressing into his jacket anymore. He glanced over his shoulder. The two men stood a good six feet behind them.

"Keep going," the man yelled.

Shawn hesitated. Why would they make them walk all this way just to shoot them in the back? How would that ever be construed as an accident? This wasn't hunting land. The snow grew thinner, smoother.

Tripping over tumbleweed, he let go of Jackie's hand on instinct to catch himself. His hands sank into the packed-down snow.

"Shawn, are you okay?" She crouched next to him.

The winds eased but still blew her hair across her face. Her vibrant blue eyes made his heart pound harder.

He'd been the one to leave her without a fight all those years ago. He knew he'd grown up a lot since his teenage years, but the thought smacked him upside the head. Why had he never realized the irony before? The very hurt he'd been running from, the very hurt he'd been trying to prevent, he'd inflicted on someone else. On Jackie. Why couldn't he have seen that before now?

Yes, she still hadn't defended him that horrible night, but he hadn't really given her a chance, had he? What if he'd stayed? It was a stupid question because he couldn't change the past. Being submerged in ice water must have frozen some of his brain cells.

His hands sank deeper in the snow. He shifted to try to get up before the men yelled another threat. Jackie offered her hand and he accepted it. As he stood, he lifted his knee and stepped into a lunge to fully stand. The earth shifted underneath his front foot. His heel slipped forward. Jackie clung tighter to his hand. "What—"

The snow shifted and started to move, like quicksand. Jackie pulled on his arm then slipped past him. She screamed. The snow disappeared beneath them and they plunged into darkness.

Stale, cold, black air engulfed them. He tightened his fingers around her hand, determined not to let go, and reached out with his other hand to grab on to anything. *Anything, please!*

His grip found a hard ledge of some sort and his fingers dug in deep, pain radiating down his forearm from the strain. His torso slammed against rock from the sudden jolt. He groaned at the impact and squinted into the dark. His feet dangled. Musty air swirled up and around him, escaping into a hole above, into the night sky.

"Jackie?"

"You can let go of me." Her voice was quiet and weak.

"What? Never." He tried to tilt his head to see her. He blinked rapidly, his eyes beginning to adjust. A mine. They had to be in a mine. A mine was always an unknown. The chute could be fifty to hundreds of feet straight down into the earth, depending on when it was built.

"It's fine," she whispered, gasping. "I think I've got something, but I need both hands."

His left arm stretched as far as it could go without his socket threatening to jump ship, but if he let go and she didn't have a good grip…

He couldn't bear the thought. "Are you sure you have footing?"

"I think so. You have to let go, Shawn. My arm can't—"

"Okay. One, two, three." Their fingers slipped apart from each other. He moved his hand to join the other on what seemed like an old piece of wood. His feet tapped the tunnel or enclosure they were in. The walls had to be made out of rock. He found a foothold that helped ease the strain on his arms and tried to catch his breath. "You still with me?"

"I think I'm fine." She broke into a coughing fit. "I'm standing on something. Where are we?"

"Shhh," he whispered. He strained his ears to listen. The men knew about this mine. That was why they'd stopped when they did. They knew they'd fall right in it. That *would* make their deaths look like an accident, and he'd walked right into the trap. They'd never have justice. But on the bright side, they were alive. They just couldn't let the men know it lest they tried harder.

Every second he clung to the side without being able to truly see his surroundings was like a python tightening around his ribs. It hurt to breathe. Finally, mercifully, he heard the slightest rev of an engine. The ground above them vibrated, dust and snow slipping past him. Were the men really gone or pulling a fast one again?

An ominous creak of metal echoed around them.

"Shawn?" Her voice wavered.

He pulled out the phone from his pocket and clicked the side button so the screen would light up their surroundings. His hand looked more like a claw gripping on to a rung of an old wooden ladder, but he was hanging straight down while the ladder was attached diagonally, as was the mine chute. He shifted to balance his foot on a ladder rung. He twisted carefully, and the wood creaked with every movement.

He tilted the light in her direction, this time flicking on the flashlight app for a more concentrated beam. Jackie clung to another partial slat of wood that served as a framework for the chute, but her feet rested on the trunk of a blue car, pointed vertically down into the earth. The car groaned and shifted, testing whatever rock formations temporarily suspended it.

She glanced down at her feet and cried out. "It's my car!"

A couple of creaks echoed through the air. She screamed as the car plunged a few inches, and she barely was able to keep her fingers on the wood frame. Shawn dropped the phone as he reached for her. The light bounced all around the rock tunnel as he spun on the ladder and tried again, reaching for her with his other arm. He grabbed her wrist. "Let go of the wood!"

She looked up, her eyes wide. The car creaked against the rock again.

His phone had landed on the rearview window of the car. The light illuminated the inside of the vehicle and reflected off a construction vest on a dead man who was pressed in between the windshield and the dashboard. Shawn fought against a wave of nausea. He didn't know the man well, but he'd been the associate field manager for the geothermal site. He had to be whose murder she'd witnessed in the first place.

Metal groaned again.

The walls of the tunnel shifted enough that rocks and debris sprinkled on them from every direction. "Jackie!"

She let go of the wood and her other hand grabbed his arm. She dangled from his grip, but he couldn't let go of the ladder, despite the snow falling onto the back of his neck from above. He strained the muscles in his back, pulling her toward him. One of her feet found a foothold on the wall, and her other leg stretched to find a rung on the ladder.

A squeal of metal breaking apart pierced the air, and the car plunged. All the air rushed out of him in shock. The car must've dropped fifty, a hundred feet down. If not for his lost phone, they'd only see darkness. Jackie climbed up his arm. He had to stay bent over until she managed to get both feet on the ladder. She wrapped one arm around his right ankle. "You can let go of my hand now."

"The ladder could go at any minute. Keep hanging on to my ankle." He let go of her and moved to climb up the ancient wood.

"Okay. Let's climb together. Move your right foot first."

He did and her fingers stayed wrapped around his ankle. He could feel her movement on the ladder. They moved in slow motion during the precarious climb, until the tunnel curved enough that he could see how they'd slid down.

"It's like the world's worst underground slide," she said.

"Something like that. An abandoned mine." He reached the top rung. "Okay. This is the hard part."

"You've got to be kidding me. Please don't tell me we haven't done the hard part yet."

"I know." He hesitated, panting, trying in vain to catch his breath. "I'm sorry. I'm going to lean over you, take the rope out of your backpack and give you one end. Then I'm going to need you to let go of my foot so I can rock climb my way out and pull you up."

"Just another day at the gym, right?" Her voice shook, but her bravado kept him going. He embraced the attitude. Just one more pull-up. He could do it.

He had to or they would both die.

She couldn't watch. The right thing to do was to encourage him, she knew that, but internally she was screaming. More rocks bounced past her and she bit her lip. Shawn groaned and she finally lifted her chin.

His feet dangled above her before he maneuvered over the final ledge and climbed out of the hole that had sucked them inside. The quiet and darkness of the mine seemed to amplify the moment she was left alone.

The packed-down snow area she'd thought was from snowmobiles had to be the earlier work of those men on ATVs, especially the one with the plow. They'd tried to cover up the death of the man she'd seen murdered by putting him in her car.

Her breathing turned shallow. If they succeeded at killing her, how likely would it be that her family would ever find her?

"I think I've got the rope secure," Shawn called out. "Test it without letting go."

Not exactly the best pep talk she'd heard. She closed her eyes and lifted up what seemed like the hundredth prayer for help. She twisted a section of the rope around and around her forearm and gripped it as she shifted.

"So far so good. Keep going. I'm holding it, too."

She took another tentative step and the wood cracked but held. Each step challenged her trust in God, the rope and Shawn. She reached the ladder's top rung and dared to look up. The space between the ladder and the ground above might as well have been hundreds of feet because she didn't see how she could climb it.

Shawn took a deep breath, sprawled on his stomach in the mouth of the mine, his arms hanging down and holding the rope with both hands. The sight was enough to make her want to scream in frustration. "What's to keep *you* from sliding down again?"

"I've got the middle part of the rope around my leg, and the last bit wrapped around a boulder. Ready when you are, Jackie."

She held on to the rope tightly and stared right into his eyes as she stepped off the ladder, launching off the same foothold Shawn had found earlier. He let go of the rope with one hand and grabbed the back of her backpack. The brief halt to gravity pulling her back down was enough to find another foothold and press up. A moment later she collapsed onto the firm ground and cried out. Every fiber of her muscles felt like it had been stretched and pulled.

"Are you hurt?" Shawn checked her over, helping her stand. As soon as they were far enough away from the mine, he untied the middle of the rope that had been looped around his foot and freed the end tied around a boulder.

She groaned at the effort her abs required for her

to get back to her knees. "I told you I never wanted to be out here again. I never wanted to be a survivalist." She wasn't sure if she was talking more to Shawn or the Lord.

"I know, but we can't focus on that right now." He reached for her hand, still gasping for breath, as well. "Come on, Jackie. I can't do this without you."

"Since when?" she asked. "You said you like to rely only on yourself. You don't want to be needed, and here I am, utterly dependent."

"I never said I didn't want to help people, and we need each other."

She shook her head, unwilling to process what he was saying. She couldn't hold on to the pain in silence any longer. It all hurt. Physically, emotionally, mentally, she felt desperate to give up. To stop feeling pain.

She sucked in a breath and hated the cold air she had to breathe. "I can't do this. I can't. Did you see him? The man? Dead Geothermal Plant Employee Found in Journalist's Vehicle in a—" Her voice trembled. "What'd you say it was? A mine? I can't even finish the headline. And even if I could, it would be too long. Just like this entire weekend. It's too much."

Her heart rate and mouth wouldn't slow down. They'd almost died. Never again. She'd promised herself she'd never again be in a situation like this. And yet here she was.

"Yes," he said solemnly.

"Is that all you can say?"

"His name was Bob, and he was the associate field manager." Shawn walked farther away from the hole and beckoned her to follow him. "Some mines go straight down like a chute or are hidden in rocks like that. Just breathe, Jackie. You've been amazing. I need you to hang on a little longer."

She wasn't in the right mindset to listen to encouragement. When she'd seen the dead body in her car, she'd reached her breaking point. "I thought you knew this area. Didn't you know about the mine?"

"If I had, there would've been wire sealing off the entrance and a giant orange sign that said Stay Out, Stay Alive." He threw his arms up in the air and exhaled. "There are hundreds—thousands, maybe—of abandoned mines we haven't found yet. Ancient. You know that." He dropped his hands and his shoulders rounded. She saw then. He was shaken, too.

The wind gusted and seemed to suck out the air from her lungs. "You're right. I'm sorry I'm letting all this get to me." The snow pelted her face without any sign of stopping.

"What worries me most is whoever we're dealing with knows the land better than I do." He dropped to his knees.

"What are you doing?" She realized they'd been following their footsteps back to the tree line. "We have to keep moving. It's too late to stop. Let's get to the other side. Sturdy rock over there, remember? Are you okay?"

He froze and looked up. He lifted his gun. "Much better now." He stood and holstered his weapon.

A light flashed in the distance. "Was that light going or coming?"

"I can't be sure. Let's assume they turned a corner. Please, follow me."

She held up a hand. "We should use the rope now, right? We don't know when one of us could fall through another snow bridge."

He hesitated to answer.

"Is it a bad idea?"

He shook his head. "No." He tied the rope around her waist. "I'm scared, though. If I fall, you go down with me. I can't stomach seeing you hurt," he said softly.

She stared at him in confusion. What had happened to the man who wanted to go everything alone? He turned away from her and they pressed on. Once they reached the trail the ATVs had taken, she forced herself into a jog to get across.

Shawn kept glancing back, his face turned into the wind, to check on her, and she waved him ahead. There was no use talking. The weather wouldn't let him hear her even if she shouted. The cloud shifted and the moon got its chance to light up the sky. The snowflakes dissipated.

They reached the rocky plateau. It had a downhill slant just as he'd told her to expect. She took another step and her leg gave out, sending her tumbling into the snow.

Shawn jogged back, his hands outstretched. "Are you okay?"

Her cheeks burned from the wind and the heat of embarrassment. She trained to stay physically fit, but never before had she asked her body to endure so much. "Aside from needing a massage and a hot shower, I'm peachy." She glanced down at her pants. They were almost soaked through. His were, as well. If they didn't get to some warmth soon, they would both be facing the real threat of frostbite. "My boots don't have the best traction."

The light bounced again and she studied the trajectory of the beams. "They're definitely coming back this way already."

"We spent a lot of time getting out of that mine."

Although they'd made it across and above the trail to the plateau, they would still be in perfect line of sight as soon as the vehicles curved around the final bend. The moon and stars to the east provided enough light to make out a shadowed line of shapes farther down the hill, though it was hard to see in between the gusts of blowing snow. "Shawn, there's nowhere to hide."

"I know." He turned to her. "What would Wolfe Dutton do?"

She barked a laugh. "Oh, the cold *really* must be getting to you to ask that."

"I'm trained in survival skills but not running for my life. You and your dad had the imagination to come up with all sorts of scenarios for his show and how to get out of it."

"I don't know what my dad would do. He never did an episode like this."

"So forget that. What would Jackie Dutton do?"

She reared back in surprise. "What?"

"The only idea I have is burying ourselves in the snow before they round those next two bends and see us."

"You're so determined to make a snow cave! But

we're soaked in wet clothes with no hope of drying off, and digging enough room would take too long."

"The worst thing hikers can do is press on in the darkness, especially in a storm," he fired back.

"Most hikers don't have other men hunting them down."

"So we run and hope they don't notice us."

"We can't travel that much distance that fast by foot." She knew what he was doing with the rapid-fire exchange. Forcing a debate, challenging her, encouraging the best in her to rise up. She pushed away all other emotions and focused on the danger at hand, and she knew what they had to do. "Glissade."

The term was really a fancy way to say they needed to go sledding without a sled. His eyes widened and he looked behind him at the thick rock plateau that took them straight downhill for a good mile. "We don't have an ice ax to slow us down. We could go too fast and not be able to stop and—"

"And die," she finished for him. But if they stayed put, they would surely die, as well. She moved her backpack to the front, putting it on backward so the padding covered her chest. If they slid down, she didn't want her pack being ripped off of her from the speed. "I don't see any other way. Do you? We're exhausted, our clothes are wet…"

"The angle could be deceptive. We still have ropes around our—"

"If one of us goes off course, then the other has a chance to stop them."

"Agreed. It's the best idea we've got." He sat down in the snow, his legs slightly bent. "It's now or never.

As soon as we get to that line of trees, we do everything in our power to brake."

She sat beside him and made sure her pants, even though damp, were still tucked into her boots. "Let's pray there's not another abandoned mine."

"I've already prayed that prayer." He nodded gravely. "Say when. Any second and they're going to see us."

She leaned back ever so slightly. The snow proved packable, and if not for the horrible conditions and utter exhaustion, the break in the weather would be ideal for a snowman. "Now."

A slight shove-off with her hands proved all that was necessary with a sloped terrain. She picked up speed at a surprising rate. She tucked her chin in as snow pelted her from every angle. Faster and faster. They had to be pushing over thirty miles an hour at this rate. The shapes in the distance came into focus. The trees approached rapidly.

She pressed her heels down deeper, hoping to slow down, but instead, her pace increased. She threw her legs and arms out wide, clawing the snow with her heels and fingers. She dared a look to her left.

Shawn lifted his right arm, clearly struggling with the sheer speed, as well, but he pointed. He shouted a word she couldn't hear, but there was no questioning that he was trying to tell her to go to the trees. He twisted, falling over onto his side, which forced his legs to point in her direction. He slid diagonally, right for her.

If she didn't make adjustments, he'd barrel right into her. Or the rope that connected them would make her go that way whether she wanted to or not. She mimicked his movements, but a wrong calculation would mean slamming into a tree, which at this speed would break bones or worse.

TWELVE

Shawn aimed his trajectory for one lone tree that stood a good twenty feet away from the other thicker grouping. Satisfied with the angle, he flopped back onto his back. The snow pelted him from every direction. At this speed, the flakes felt like sand pelting his face.

He squinted through the blowing snow. If he aimed left of the tree and Jackie aimed right, it would catch the rope in the middle and force them to stop. But not necessarily before they hit the rest of the trees.

Either way, this was going to hurt.

Shawn flipped over onto his stomach and dug his arms and feet deeper into the snow. Mercifully, his speed slowed. Hopefully Jackie was doing whatever she could to slow down, too. He dug his feet in deeper. His speed decreased. The low branches of the tree slapped his back. They'd passed the tree. *Please*...

The snow thickened, hardened, underneath the north side of the tree. His knees objected, as if sliding along a hardwood floor. He gritted his teeth against the discomfort. Slower, slower. Pressure tugged at his waist from the rope hanging up on the tree trunk, but he stopped, panting, shivering, before the rope dug deep. He flipped over onto his back. The evergreen trees wore thick white scarves made of snow on each row of branches. The clouds above them parted enough to show the most dazzling spectacle of glittering stars.

The snow insulated him from the wind for a brief moment. He heard Jackie's movements nearby.

"What if this is the last Christmas we ever have?" she asked.

That was the last thing he'd expected to hear from her. "What? Don't talk like that." He jumped up to a crouch and ran toward her.

"We might not survive, so it could be. My favorite Christmas memories are walking into the dark living room with nothing shining but the lights on the Christmas tree and dawn's first light barely seeping through the windows."

He reached her and took a knee, worried she'd hit her head, as she hadn't moved from her sprawled position in the snow. "Are you okay? We've descended far enough they shouldn't be able to see us."

"What was your favorite Christmas memory?" She shivered and held her stomach tightly. The rope tied around her waist had likely bruised her, and he realized she was buying time to recover before she needed to move. He would do anything to have her home right this minute, but he knew he had more to ask of her if they were going to make it to safety.

"Your parents gave good gifts. I still have the multitool your dad gave me. Made to last," he said.

She raised an eyebrow. "Really? That's your favorite memory?"

He exhaled. "Fine. Christmas dinner. I liked the way everyone teased each other but in a good-natured way." Those dinners were the only time he'd witnessed how a real family interacted.

She gave a self-satisfied smile. "Knew it." Her smile dropped.

"Jackie, be honest. Are you okay?"

She waved him away, her hand still on her stomach. "I will be. I have to be. Just give me another second. Pretend we're in a snow cave." Her smile wobbled and she pointed at the trees above, from her position in the snow. "Someone once told me that Martin Luther walked home one Christmas Eve and became stunned by the beauty of the shimmering tree in the moonlight. He went home that night and decorated a fir tree with small candles. I don't know if it's historically accurate, but it's easy to believe. The snow does glisten like little lights from this angle. It's beautiful."

Shawn held out his hands and helped her to a seated position, though he wasn't ready to let go of her. "I thought we have Christmas trees because the branches are pointing upward and the evergreen tree reminds us of eternal life."

"Whatever the reason, I'd just like to imagine this one is *my* Christmas tree."

He pointed to the tallest one in the middle. "This one? Good choice. You can see it from the valley below. I hope every year that no one gets a permit to cut it down." The adrenaline faded ever so slightly, even though his heart continued to pump as if running a marathon.

A star rocketed through the midnight sky to the east. "Do you think the wise men were glad they didn't have to follow *that* star?"

He laughed. "Okay, now I'm worried about what the cold is doing to *your* brain." He tugged gently on her hands. "Time to get up, out of the snow. Not much farther now."

"The cold is winning, that's what it's doing to me." She groaned as she stood and moved the backpack from her chest to her back. The wind whistled around them, but the tree provided just enough shelter to catch their breath.

He stared into her eyes, also glistening from the reflection of the stars. It was like his heart had been dormant in a winter slumber for ages, and despite the freezing storm about to attack them, his heart seemed determined to thaw in her presence. "I've always known you were amazing, Jackie, but I'm reminded over and over just how much."

Her eyes softened. Even with her wet hair and red cheeks, she radiated beauty from the inside out. She stepped closer and opened her mouth to reply when their Christmas tree exploded in bullets.

"No!"

Shawn covered his arms over her head as they both cowered. They'd been too late, then. The men on the ATVs had spotted them from above. An intense wind gust swayed another tree in their direction. Snow flew up in their faces. He grabbed Jackie's hand and tugged her deeper into the trees. "Stay down." They brushed in between two trees, and a second later, another gun-shot cracked the branches.

"I'm trying not to touch the branches," Jackie yelled.

"More concerned about the bullets touching us at the moment."

He spotted a drop-off point. It might not have been the one he was initially thinking of, but he didn't have the time or lighting to find the best vantage point. He turned to the closest tree and searched for the thickest branch.

He pressed his boot into the needles and hopped on the branch until it bent down. Jackie offered an arm to help him balance, and he kicked at the weakest point of the branch, until it snapped off.

Her eyes widened. "Are you serious? We're trying a snow anchor?"

She understood his intention. Good. "The drop-off point is too far away from the trees, but we are angled away from the path the ATVs must be on. I think if we time it right, we can get off the cliff without being shot," he said.

"But the snow? Do you think it will hold us?"

"You saw how it packed."

She closed her eyes. "Okay."

"No other ideas?" If she didn't debate him, that actually gave him peace. It meant it really was the best idea they had.

"None. I can't believe I'm *choosing* to go over a cliff this time. Has to be better than doing so by accident, right?"

Man, he loved this woman. The unbidden thought stole his breath before the wind could. He couldn't process it right now. "They appear to have stopped shooting for the moment, but that might be because they're headed this way. Keep your head down in case I'm wrong and they shoot." He'd been wrong more times than he'd like to admit, but he prayed that this time he'd guessed right.

He rushed forward into the open snow and stopped two feet short of the edge, in case he fell victim to a snow bridge or another cornice. He dug frantically in the snow, until about a foot down.

Jackie reached his side, anxiously scanning the tops of the trees in front of them. She dropped to her knees. "We're doing the T-Trench snow anchor?"

"Yeah." He grabbed the rope between them and slipped it on the middle of the stick before he shoved the stick underneath the lip of snow he'd packed down. Jackie rapidly refilled the trench from the back edge while Shawn made a much thinner trench on the top of the snow for the rope to follow.

Engine noises carried through the wind. "I'm really beginning to dislike that sound," he muttered. He looked up. "You ready?"

She hopped over the trench area and they checked their ropes, together. She dropped to her knees, eyes closed. "Lord, be with us."

"Amen." He threw the extra rope over the side, even though the ends were still tied to their waists. They would need to work their way down to the end. They dropped to their stomachs, stuck their legs out behind them, both holding on to their sides of the rope, and began inching backward.

Jackie stopped for a second and removed a six-inch

branch from within her hair. "I never thought I'd have a love-hate relationship with pine."

"Those are spruce. Both trees have vitamin C but pine tea tastes more like turpentine. Spruce isn't too bad. Motivation to tell the difference."

She laughed but kept inching backward. "Keep talking. I prefer to think we're doing a crazy stunt than running away from men who want to kill us and throw us into a mine."

His feet met air and he stilled for a moment. She gasped as hers did, as well. "Stay there a second."

He tugged on the rope. So far the trench anchor had worked. "Here goes." He slid down farther, always keeping a hand on the rope. He dropped, his body fully away from the edge, and swung with the wind until his feet pushed against the rock wall, taking some of the sting off his shoulders and arms. He stuck his legs out so he was sitting on air and glanced down. The moon weaved in and out of visibility but he spotted the cement pads and drilling equipment below them. They just needed to get to that control room and call for help.

Now, if only he could guarantee they didn't run out of rope before they reached the bottom.

The moment her feet reached air she wanted to cry out. She enjoyed rock climbing. Indoors with fake rock and a padded floor below, though, and only after she'd been sedentary for the rest of the day at work. Hanging by a rope, being tossed about by gusts of wind after her body had already been tested to its limits, was not the same thing.

She fought between wanting to use her feet as a

clamp around the rope, which would take the brunt of most of her body weight, and needing her feet to keep her far away from slamming into rock. Each time the wind stilled, she'd lean back as far as possible, both hands gripped around the rope. She relaxed her palms and feet just enough to slide down as rapidly as possible. She felt Shawn's hands as he grabbed her ankles and pulled her closer to the rock face, wordlessly.

She slid down at a slower pace, not understanding why he wanted her so close to the rock face until his hands grabbed her waist. She let go and he set her down on the ground. If he hadn't pulled her, she would've landed in a thicket of some sort.

His fingers worked rapidly on the knots around her waist. "Quietly," he whispered, his lips against her hair. That was when she spotted the flickering light just past the cement pads. Freed of the rope, Shawn's arms moved lightning fast, pulling the rope until it fell completely from above and dropped at their feet. She turned around so he could stuff it back in her pack rapidly. The wind whistled so hard now she could hardly hear herself think, but she thought an engine roared nearby.

His fingers reached for her hand. "Work our way around to the control building. Stay close to the rock."

They made it about ten feet, single file, behind prickly bushes poking into their arms and legs, when a giant beam of light bounced on the rock above them, narrowly missing them. "Shawn, they have those radios, remember? Someone down here is helping the gunmen on the plateau look for us."

He grumbled. "Great."

Two steps forward, the rock wall had a five-foot-tall vertical crevice, maybe two feet wide. "Can you fit in there?"

Without discussing it, he ducked, twisted sideways and stepped inside. She followed him wordlessly. The air seemed warmer and drier than she'd expect. Whether from the break in wind or the geothermal heat, she didn't know. She didn't care. She wanted more warmth and for her nose to stop feeling like an ice cube, despite her efforts at keeping the lower half of her face tucked in the coat. Another larger, wider crevice opened up to the left.

Shawn stepped into the space. "This way the light won't catch us. Seems this cave winds deeper, but how about we stop here for a minute while they look?"

He guided her steps in the darkness until they fitted snugly, facing each other, in a narrow space. "I hope there aren't any hungry animals hiding in there."

"Do you have your Taser handy?"

She twisted to unzip the backpack and slipped the Taser into her coat pocket, but her forehead bumped against his chest in the process. She readjusted the backpack and faced him. "Sorry."

He leaned over and kissed her forehead as if to say it was okay. She didn't mind, though. They'd just been through a lot together and were so close to the nightmare ending. It was perfectly normal to show some sort of affection. Especially in the form of a friendly kiss to the forehead that didn't mean anything.

The warmth of his breath moved to her cheek. Her heart jolted and her breath caught. She was scared to believe the kiss to the forehead meant more. He kissed her cheek. She closed her eyes. Just as she was about to ask him what he was doing, his lips brushed gently over her mouth.

Heat rushed through her of an entirely different kind. Her hands reached for the front of his coat and she pulled him closer. His arms wrapped around her shoulders and his kiss deepened. Light flickered through her closed eyes.

They broke apart. Where could it be coming from? Deeper within the rock wall, the light reflected a second time, except it wasn't originating from the initial crevice they'd entered. There went their chance at talking about that kiss.

"Shawn?" she whispered. The flicker illuminated an orange cord wrapped tightly around the curve of rock. She looked down at her feet and spotted it behind her heel, weaving all the way outside. The light intensified into more of a glow around the corner. A shadow crossed it, interrupting the beam. Shawn looked at both the entrance to the cave and the corner. She imagined he was debating their options. She didn't have anything constructive to offer.

Her mind, body and heart were reeling from the last few days, especially the past few minutes. Her skin felt raw from the wind, in a way similar to the blistering sensation from a sunburn. Ironic. She desperately wanted to change clothes or get a warm blanket. The temperature had dipped enough that the snow had stuck to her trousers in clumps, frozen, not melting but still there, ensuring she would stay chilled even with shelter over her head.

Maybe the glow around the corner meant warmth.

The crevice also had flickering lights. They were trapped. The light outside definitely came from the gunmen, but the light from within was still a mystery. Shawn turned and tiptoed toward the glow. At the corner he waved her back. He removed the gun from his holster and held it up to his chin.

Jackie stayed behind him but followed his example by holding the trigger of the Taser, though she kept her hand within the coat pocket, as the dry warmth of the pocket was too tempting to give up. She kept her eyes on the opening to the outdoors, lest someone sneak up on them.

Shawn peeked his head around the corner. "Pete?" Shawn's voice came out in a whisper. Without giving Jackie enough time to react, Shawn strode around the corner. "Pete!" He didn't quite shout, but his loud whisper bounced around the cave.

Jackie hustled around the corner after him. A man wearing the Bureau's winter uniform crouched in front of a light the size of a basketball, with a small chisel and a brush in his hand. Presumably, this was Pete the archaeologist. The dirt around him had been excavated into a perfectly square recessed floor, with various pots and artifacts covered in dust on their side. A squat statue roughly a foot high sat right in front of him.

The man stiffened. "Shawn?" His eyes widened, and he frowned, then straightened out of his crouch to standing.

"Are you okay?" Shawn asked. He put his gun back in the holster, but kept his hand on it as he approached. "Have they hurt you?"

"Uh…no. But you shouldn't be here. It's not safe."

"Yeah, neither should you. How long have they had you?" Shawn shook his head, staring at the artifacts. "I knew they were looters. Come on. You can tell us on our way out."

A space heater across the room practically put her feet on autopilot. The orange power cord had split into other extension cords. The engine sound she'd heard earlier had to be from a generator. She stood in front of the heater, as close as she could without setting her clothes on fire, as Pete set down the tools in the dirt and licked his lips. "I've lost track of time. Listen, they're always watching the entrance. I don't know how you got in, but you should leave while you have a chance."

Shawn reached his hand out for Pete to grab. "You're right, but you're coming with us. We have a plan."

Pete hesitated for half a second, and Jackie might've imagined it but she thought Pete glanced at Shawn's gun before he nodded. Maybe he wanted to make sure Shawn could deliver on his promises before taking a chance at escape. She'd seen firsthand evidence that the gunmen out there—especially the bald man—had no problem killing to suit their needs. If Pete thought the safest answer was to do what the looters wanted, though, he was sorely mistaken. "I saw one of those men murder someone," she said. "And they've been trying to kill me ever since, likely because I'm a witness. You've probably seen too much, as well, Mr. Wooledge. Give those men what you want, and they still might kill you."

The click of a gun sent chills up her spine.

"Finally, a smart girl. I get so tired of people underestimating me. Too bad for you that you came back to test me." The bald man, the one who'd killed the employee, aimed his weapon right at her chest.

THIRTEEN

Shawn stepped in front of Jackie in one move, his gun pointing at the man. "Bureau ranger. Drop your weapon."

"No!" Pete waved his hands in front of Shawn.

The gunman frowned at Pete. "What are you—"

"Don't shoot them," Pete interrupted. "I promised I'd finish the job. If you shoot them, I'll stop helping you. You'd have to kill me."

The man squinted hard at Pete, his weapon still trained on Shawn, as if weighing his options. "Fine. If he puts down his weapon."

Pete caught Shawn's eyes and nodded, as if he had his own plan that Shawn should follow. He felt Jackie's fingers grasping the back of his coat. She stayed close to him, closer than usual. "Don't do it," she whispered.

He didn't trust the gunman any more than Jackie did, but he also didn't see another solution. If he tried to shoot, the gunman might still get off a shot and hit Pete or Jackie. The man stepped closer. "I agree not to kill you and the girl if you drop your weapon. What will it be?"

Shawn set down his weapon and kicked it over, hoping the man would stay away from Jackie. The man picked up the gun. "You two sit down. Against the wall." He waved the gun at Pete. "Come here. A word."

Jackie slipped behind Shawn and angled herself on his left side, closest to the gunman. She pressed herself so closely into his side that he had no choice but to put his right arm around her shoulder as they sank to the ground, all eyes on Pete approaching the gunman. "I don't trust him," she muttered, barely loud enough for Shawn to hear.

No surprise. He didn't trust the gunman, either. If he'd killed Bob, the associate field manager, and Darrell, the detectorist, there'd be nothing to prevent him from killing all of them once they were out of an area that could ricochet bullets. Jackie moved her right arm diagonally to her left shoulder and grabbed his hand that was resting there, as if she wanted to hold hands.

The motion surprised him but he eagerly held her hand. He hoped with one squeeze she understood how sorry he was that he'd failed. His declaration that he'd only rely on himself, that unconditional love wasn't for him, seemed so foolish now. He'd wasted his time shielding himself, under the delusion that as long as he took care of the land, he'd be satisfied enough. Two days of time with Jackie, the woman who despite the years gone by still knew him best, and his heart felt renewed and desperate to have a chance to live life to its fullest. But there was nothing in his own wisdom that he could do. They'd lost and would have to rely only on God and the hope that the gunman would make a mistake.

Jackie didn't seem to get any of that sentiment from their brief moment of handholding. In fact, she seemed annoyed. She tugged at his fingers, sliding his hand down the side of her arm. He finally understood what she was trying to communicate when she placed his hand at the side of her waist. His fingers brushed against the hard plastic outline of something in her pocket.

The Taser! She was trying to get his hand close to her pocket where she'd placed the Taser. She tilted her head and looked up at him with questions in her eyes. He couldn't explain the problem without the gunman hearing, though. If the man still had a gun pointed at one of them, using the Taser inside the cave would be too dangerous. The man might be able to get a bullet or two off, especially if he was facing them, before hitting the ground.

"Get back to work," the man barked at Pete. Pete turned around, his eyes flashing with anger, but he didn't reply as he walked back toward them. The man stepped forward. "Just so you know, Carl and Spencer are on their way back here with the trailer. The blizzard has arrived and is intensifying by the minute, so this will be the final trip. No exceptions. If you know what's good for you—" his eyes darted to Shawn and Jackie before returning to Pete "—have them help."

Pete set his jaw and turned to stare at the gunman an unusually long time. The gunman raised an eyebrow, as if unsure how to make Pete do what he wanted for a moment. "I'm going to check on Carl's progress," the man said. "But I'll be right at the entrance." He waved the second gun at Shawn. "Anything suspicious and I get trigger-happy."

The moment the man had turned his back on them, Pete knelt down, as if to start working on the antiquities again, but he whispered to Shawn. "His satellite phone doesn't work in the cave—the rock walls are too thick unless he gets close to the entrance. While he's busy you can tell me—what's your plan to escape? Is it ruined now since he got your gun? Is backup on the way?"

Shawn blinked, unsure of what to say that wouldn't dash all hope. He needed Pete to stay positive and focused and not try anything stupid. Being held at gunpoint pretty much changed everything, though.

"Before we tell you," Jackie hastily said, "what surprises might we be dealing with? How did you end up here, anyway?"

"Jackie?" That same look of distrust she'd flashed at him all those years ago appeared in her eyes now, except it was aimed at Pete. And why did she insinuate they still had a plan to escape? With a gunman blocking their only route, there was little chance they could get to the control room anymore and call for help. Even if they were able to stealthily take away the man's satellite phone, they would need to get outside for it to work.

"He can tell us while he works." Jackie leaned forward, away from the rock wall, and offered a small, encouraging smile to Pete. Shawn was baffled at her response but stayed silent.

Pete looked over his shoulder, making sure the

gunman was still far enough away. "You know Bob Hutchison, the associate field manager?"

Shawn felt a little sick. "Not well," he said. Though it was enough to recognize the man's profile, dead, in Jackie's car.

"During the feasibility and impact study required before approving the geothermal permit, he found this place. He apparently realized what he'd stumbled on—"

"And what's that?" Jackie asked.

Pete flashed Shawn a questioning look as if asking why he should talk to Jackie. He was tempted to apologize for her natural journalistic tendencies, but he'd give her a few more minutes because her instinct seemed right. The more they knew about what they were dealing with, the better they could plan an escape. Though they were running out of time. If those ATVs turned around off the plateau and came back on the corridor path, they had minutes to spare before more gunmen arrived.

"An Oregon Trail campsite," Pete answered. "For whatever reason, maybe illness, lightening their load or an ambush outside of the cave, they left a vast number of items behind. Once the looters Bob had hired started digging, though, we found an entirely new layer underneath." He gestured behind him. "Tribal antiquities. Untouched stonework—I'd have to guess from the 1300s."

Pete's eyes lit up. "If this weren't for looters, I'd be thrilled at the discovery. I'm not ready to say which tribe, but I know enough to recognize this statue is the crowning jewel. At least half a million dollars for her alone. I've almost got her free." Pete blinked rapidly. "Anyway, Bob realized the dig was bigger than anticipated, so he started sabotaging the construction to give him more time without being discovered. I got curious, found out what he was doing, and before I knew it, I was a hostage."

"How many other looters? Gunmen, specifically," Shawn asked.

Pete shrugged. "Can't say for sure. They kept me working."

"We know there's three for sure." The radio squawked, and Shawn held a finger over his mouth for a moment to listen, but he couldn't hear the conversation at the edge of the cave. Frustration built. "Have you counted more?"

"Did you know the assistant field manager was murdered?" Jackie interjected.

Pete raised an eyebrow, but it seemed more out of irritation than surprise. "Like I said, the site was more lucrative than Bob realized. The looters disagreed with how he was managing things and killed him." He turned to Shawn. "It was a sad day."

Jackie leaned forward, away from Shawn's arm. "So the storm approaching worked in their favor, right? They knew the park and all the roads would be closed. They could make multiple trips with the trailer and ATVs and never be spotted or tracked. Up until the storm, during the construction, they'd been stashing everything at your field trailer, right? Which is perfect, because no one would suspect artifacts in a Bureau trailer would be stolen property."

Pete shifted uncomfortably. "They took me hostage. I don't know what they were doing or planning."

Shawn nodded. "So the three gunmen we've spotted is all you know about?"

"Yes, yes, that sounds right."

"You didn't know what they were doing in your own field trailer?" Jackie placed her left hand down on the ground and moved to a crouched position. "The sabotage has been going on quite some time, so the looting had to have started before that. Right? That's what you said."

"They weren't at my field trailer before this storm." He shrugged. "When are you going to answer my question? Is help on the way?"

"What about the boss?" she fired back.

Shawn's pulse raced at the way she was questioning him, almost as if it was more an interrogation than an interview. A crunch of shoes on rocks pulled his attention. The gunman rounded the corner and walked toward them, carrying a radio in one hand and a gun in the other.

"Or maybe I'm looking at the boss." Jackie lowered her voice to a whisper. "Let's speak plainly. There's no way you think we're getting out of here alive, is there, Pete?"

Shawn reared back. "Jackie, the man's a hostage and my friend—" But the moment he said the words, pieces that hadn't made sense started clicking into place. Was she really insinuating that Pete was the one in charge of the looting? Could it be true?

He had a sinking feeling that it was too late to matter. A bullet cracked through the air. A sharp searing pain threw him backward and he slammed against the dirt floor, gasping for air.

Jackie sprinted forward. The Taser had met the mark. She hadn't realized the gunman would be able to get off a shot when the darts made contact, but at least he'd been way off on his aim. Five seconds. She had only five seconds to disarm him.

She shoved the Taser in her pocket and stomped on the man's wrist until he released the gun. Then she kicked it away. She leaned forward and grabbed the gun he'd taken from Shawn, which he'd stuck in his front waistband. She then leaped five feet away to pick up the kicked gun before the man could move to attack her.

Both guns now in her hands, she spun, arms wide to point one weapon at Pete and the other at the bald man on the ground. Pete glared at her from the floor, his hand covering his jaw, as if considering whether to take her down himself or not. She needed to know if he was hiding a weapon. He wasn't wearing bulky winter clothing like Shawn and her, but she needed to be sure. She pointed the gun at him. "Hands up, Pete."

"I'm an innocent victim here," he said. "Just ask Shawn. Hand me the other gun. I'll help." She swiveled her attention to Shawn, but he seemed to be having a cramp of some sort. He was sitting up, bent over, groaning—

He lifted his head, and in a gap between his open coat, she saw blood seeping through his shirt from a circle on the left side of his chest. She gasped and ran for him. "No!" She lifted the back of his coat. Nothing. The bullet was still inside him and could have ricocheted to other organs.

She dropped the hem, her heart rate racing. She still had to keep an eye on the gunman, who was sitting up, and Pete, whom she didn't trust despite his claims of innocence. After all her years of interviews, she could tell when a story was being fabricated. His details and timeline didn't add up.

And there *was* a boss. The bald man had mentioned one on the radio when they were stuck on that ledge. Besides, Pete had slipped in his story and had said "we found" before he'd got to the hostage bit. More than that, her gut told her he wasn't to be trusted.

She took a knee in front of Shawn. "I'm so sorry. So sorry. It's my fault."

He didn't answer. He moved his left hand up to cover the wound. Of course, he had first-aid training. He'd know what to do, but he might not be thinking straight. She pressed her two fingers against his neck. He flinched. "Cold," he muttered.

Yes, and they'd lost a lot of the sensitivity to touch. She wasn't ready to think about frostbite yet, but mercifully, she felt the warm pumping under his chin. Too rapid. That was to be expected, but the bullet had entered his chest. Even if it didn't hit the heart directly, the pathway would open up a large destructive tunnel in the cavity and could have injured tissue dangerously close to the organ.

"Jackie," he croaked. "Handcuffs."

She stared at him a second before understanding what he was talking about. She handed him the second gun. He propped his right arm up with his knee so it was pointed at the man thirty feet away. She found the pouch on Shawn's holster that held his cuffs. "Good idea. Keep pressure on your wound. We're going to get out of here, Shawn. You just have to hold on a little longer."

She turned and pointed at Pete. "Hands up."

He balked. "You have to be kidding. You're tying me up? Shawn, tell her."

"He doesn't need to tell me. I've got his back," she said. "And right now that means if you're innocent, then we'll figure it out soon enough."

"You basically shot him."

She tried not to cringe. "Yeah, well, Shawn already knows I make mistakes."

Shawn coughed. Or maybe it was a laugh. She couldn't afford to look yet.

"And you still want to handcuff me? How about taking care of the actual criminals first?"

"Stop talking, Pete," she said.

Once he had his hands on the back of his head, she twisted each wrist until she'd placed them in handcuffs, careful to watch for any signs he would put up a fight. She wasn't as smooth as she'd like, but at least she knew the basics after taking a citizen's police academy class a few years ago.

The gunman, roughly twenty feet away, pushed himself from sitting to standing, pulling out the Taser darts still attached to his chest. She pointed her weapon at him. "If I were you, I'd sit back down on your knees. I'm an even better aim with a real gun."

He sneered but did as she asked. Jackie removed

the rappelling rope and used it to tie Pete's wrists together, just above the handcuffs.

"Isn't that a bit over the top?" Shawn asked. His
question came out as a groan. "You don't know for
sure he isn't a hostage."

"You don't have to talk if it hurts," she said. "Do
you have more than one pair of handcuffs?"

"No, but knots…"

"Are my specialty." She attempted to smile. "That's
what you were going to say, right? Because I may not
be my dad, but if I'm going to embrace what I'm good
at, then one of those skills would be knots." She pulled
the rope tight to check her work and used the small key
to take off the handcuffs.

She moved to approach the bald man and fought to
project a brave face. The way he'd murdered that man
so callously with the injection wasn't something she
could forget. She glanced at Shawn before she got very
close. He gave her an encouraging nod as he aimed his
gun at the man, although his knee was the only reason
the gun was propped up at all. She did the same routine, first with the handcuffs, but with him she kept
one foot resting on the back of his knee, ready to step
there forcefully if he tried anything. As soon as he
was handcuffed, she pressed the gun in his back and
grabbed the satellite phone from his pocket. She was
surprised to find a pair of keys there, maybe belonging
to his ATV? She stuffed both in her own back pocket.

Then, using the end of the singular rope she'd tied
Pete with, she tied the men to each other, with a ten-
foot gap between them. That way it wouldn't be as

easy for one to run away. Now, if she could just get to the entrance of the cave and call for help.

Shawn moaned slightly, closing his eyes briefly. She took his gun from him so he could use both hands to put pressure on his wound. The stomping of feet ahead meant visitors would be joining them. A gun in each hand, she shook with adrenaline and pushed back the intense nausea that came with extreme levels of exhaustion. She pointed one gun at Pete and the bald man and the other toward the entrance of the cave. The men called Carl and Spencer rounded the corner. Spencer pulled a gun in less than a second, aimed directly at her. Carl moved to grab his weapon.

"Don't you dare," she said, and Carl froze, his hand hovering six inches from his weapon.

"Please don't shoot," Pete said again. "I'll do what you want. It's this crazy lady."

Spencer's eyes flickered in between Pete and the other man, indecision in his gaze. And for the briefest of moments, Jackie questioned if maybe she'd interpreted Pete's testimony poorly and been wrong. "Drop your weapon," she said.

Spencer shrugged. "Maybe I'm done with the whole lot of them."

"Drop it or the statue gets it," Shawn said behind her.

Jackie took a step closer to the wall so her peripheral vision could spot Shawn while still keeping an eye on the gunmen. Shawn held the top of the statue's head. Dirt clumps were still stuck to the bottom half, and the stonework dangled precariously over a very pointy boulder.

Pete's eyes widened. "Are you crazy? You could've damaged it, pulling it out of the dirt like that. Put it down, carefully!"

"You said it's worth at least half a million dollars, right?" Jackie asked Pete.

The man tied to Pete rolled his eyes. "Give it up. You're not fooling anyone. They know you're with us. Carl and Spencer, how about untying me, shooting the whole lot of these folks and cutting our losses? We have more than enough to get a couple million for the archive of the loot."

Pete's face blanched. "The seller will only work with me."

"Guess it's time to find a new seller," the gunman said dryly.

"If I don't check in with my contact every night, your names and photos are going straight to the FBI. I'm not stupid. This was a foolproof plan." Pete twisted to Shawn. "You know me, Shawn. I'm meticulous, a visionary. I've got profit margin to cut you in on the deal."

If Carl's and Spencer's expressions provided any indicator, these men weren't on board with splitting their profits with anyone else.

"That's a problem," Jackie interjected before the men fought any more. "Because to answer your earlier question, Pete, there is a *lot* of backup on the way. That's the reason you wanted us to believe you were a hostage, right? To find out if there was any real threat on the way? Loads. Plus, I'm still holding two guns and I'm a great shot." She looked at Spencer. "You two drop your weapons and I'll let you go. You still have ATVs outside, right?"

As if in answer, the lights flickered. Once, twice, then darkness draped them all.

FOURTEEN

Shawn fought to keep his balance, but without his vision to help, he wobbled. He struggled to stop his right hand from letting go of the statue.

"She's behind me now. Don't shoot," Pete yelled.

Shawn stumbled forward, tripping over stoneware of some sort—hopefully a sturdy pot.

"No!" Pete growled. "If you dropped that statue, I'll kill you myself."

Shawn had no choice but to let go of his wound and grab the statue with both hands, gently dropping it to the dirt. He didn't care what Pete said. He cared about preserving a people's history, one that didn't belong to the archaeologist to sell to the highest bidder. Saving Jackie's life was a higher priority, though, so he didn't stop to feel around and see if he'd succeeded in keeping it in one piece.

"I still have a gun," Jackie said. "Be quiet." A second later a light illuminated her face.

The bald gunman, however, had already made his move, his leg up, his foot kicking out toward her. Shawn's fist moved on instinct, plummeting into the man's stomach. The action broke his trajectory and the man folded up, stumbling backward, the rope taking Pete with him. They fell into a mass heap. Jackie took a shaky breath. "Thank you."

"My pleasure."

She thrust the weak light from her phone to the entrance of the cave. "The other two are gone."

"Looks like they took your idea and decided to cut their losses."

She reached up and pressed on his coat. He flinched from the pain of the pressure. "Your wound."

"Jackie, we have to get somewhere safe before I can focus too much on that. Preferably the sooner the better." He almost told her about his fight against falling and passing out, but he didn't want the men to know he lacked strength.

"Well, we also need to give you the best shot." She cringed. "I didn't mean that pun. I meant the best chance at healing properly, which means you have to keep pressure on that." Shawn grabbed her hand. The pain was making him see stars in his peripheral vision.

The bald man struggled back to his feet, a challenge with his hands tied behind his back. Shawn dropped her hand and took his gun back. "The generator probably went out. If he was right and the blizzard has set in, the air intake can suck in snow and malfunction."

"Back to the original plan?"

He nodded. "The control room generator will be designed for the elements, and will have running water, central heat and insulated walls if we have to wait out the blizzard. Except, what about them?"

"We take them with us?" Jackie pulled her hair back, twisting it and tying it into a knotted bun.

Shawn hated the idea of escorting the men, but they also couldn't leave them behind. There was shelter, sure, but nothing sturdy enough to tie them to while they waited for help. For all he knew, they had other weapons hidden on the property. "I don't have any better ideas. We'll need to watch for those ATVs, though, in case they're just regrouping."

Jackie cautiously stepped on one end of the rope and slid it with her foot until she was far enough away to stoop and pick it up. "Ever heard of Wolfe Dutton?"

Pete's and the man's eyes flickered in recognition.

"Well, I don't like to brag, but he's my father, and he taught me *everything* he knows. A blizzard isn't going to stop me from shooting straight. So tread carefully. Walk in front of me. Now."

She held the phone with one hand, flashlight on. Shawn could see from the screen pointed his direction that the battery had only 7 percent left. He could also tell from the men's expressions that they didn't consider Jackie a threat no matter what she said.

"You heard her. Move," Shawn barked. He took the opportunity to stay one step in front of her, though. If they did try to pull anything, he wanted to be the one to take the brunt of it.

They stepped outside and the wind took his breath away. His muscles tightened involuntarily and the pain surrounding his wound almost made him cry out. Instead, he grunted. "Move faster. Get past the bushes."

The wind had created drifts three feet high in portions surrounding them. The majority of light from the moon and stars was dimmed by the thick clouds dumping flakes the size of quarters. Getting across a couple of acres with these men in tow would be next to impossible, especially if they decided to fight.

Jackie held up the satellite phone. "I'm not getting any signal yet." She hollered over the wind.

"Works better when you can see the sky. With a cloud cover this thick, it might take a few tries, but we'll get through eventually." He was certain of it.

She handed him the phone. "Okay, you keep trying. You know how to work these better."

They trudged on; the men in front of them seemed to be stalling. Granted, stomping through snow with their hands behind their backs probably wasn't easy. Paths left behind by the ATVs could be seen in the snow. But only ten feet away, the trailer the ATVs had been hauling earlier that day had been left behind. They likely didn't want to fight the drag a trailer created in the winds if their goal was to get away.

A sharp pain hit his stomach and his feet flew out from under him. The half a second of looking at the trailer had proved detrimental. The men had used the ropes in between them to take him down. A bullet split the howling wind once, then twice, and the world spun.

Jackie spread her feet wide and watched the men turn to her in shock. She'd fired close enough to the side of each man's face to cause them serious, but hopefully temporary, ringing in their ears. She may not enjoy practicing survival skills in the wilderness, but she still enjoyed frequent visits to an indoor shooting range.

She'd definitely succeeded with Pete, as he howled and pressed his ear against his raised shoulder.

"Get in the trailer." She had to yell to be heard over the wind. She needed them out of the way to make sure Shawn was okay. Despite her blood burning hot that they'd hurt him, the freezing temps seemed to suck all oxygen out of her lungs each time she opened her mouth, and it was a fight to refill them. And her nose stung so bad from the cold she felt certain full recovery wasn't going to be possible. She'd permanently be able to play the part of Rudolph the Red-Nosed Reindeer every Christmas without makeup.

"I'm not getting in a trailer." The bald man curled his lips in a level of disgust and contempt that almost made her shiver. She could practically hear his mind thinking of ways to kill her.

"That was your warning shot. Next time I won't waste bullets." She dragged open the trailer door and gestured inside. Shawn still wasn't moving from the ground, and it was killing her not to run to him.

Pete staggered forward, and though it took them minutes longer than it should've, the two men begrudgingly stepped into the roughly six-foot-by-nine-foot space.

"Step all the way to the back," she yelled through the wind. The moment they did, she threw the rope inside with them and moved to close the swinging door, except she needed both hands. She tried slamming it against the wind, but it was a slow process. A second before it was fully closed, she felt movement, and the trailer shifted. The men were running at the door. Her fingers shook, fighting to get the long pin into the lock. If she didn't succeed and the impact of their bodies against the door threw her to the ground, they might overtake her.

The tip of the pin got into the hole just before initial impact, enough to keep the door from opening, but the hit moved the lock mechanism and the pin slid right back out. She pushed her entire shoulder against the door as two hands joined her efforts.

"Hurry." Shawn's face looked ashen, but he pressed with all his might as she fully slid the long pin into the lock. The door vibrated again. They'd taken another pass, but now they could bruise their shoulders all they wanted, ramming into the door, without going anywhere.

"Are you okay?" She reached for him and he draped his right arm around her shoulders and leaned slightly onto her.

"I think I fainted. Can't say it won't happen again."

"Keep pressure on the wound." She swung around, frantic to find any signs of the ATV the gunman would've been driving. The gust carried the loose snow into a whiteout in front of her. The clouds shifted ever so slightly and the moon reflected off metal in the bushes, twenty or thirty feet ahead. "Stay there."

"We might lose each other," he called. He grabbed her hand. "I'm okay with losing the men who tried to kill us. I'm not okay with losing you."

The way he looked in her eyes brought her more warmth than physically possible in the conditions. "Okay." She didn't want to argue. But she also feared he wasn't going to last much longer on his feet before he fainted again or worse. "Only if you lean on me. And try calling with the phone again."

He agreed with a nod. He held up the phone to his ear. "Ranger Shawn Burkett requesting emergency assistance," he shouted over the wind. He groaned and dropped the phone. "Only lasted a few seconds before it cut off." He looked up and the thick cloud cover had returned. "Our best chance is the landline in the control building."

"Then let's get there." She took his right hand and matched his stride. Her left foot had to move with his right foot to enable them to step in sync. They needed the momentum to step through some of the deeper snow. Finally they reached the ATV.

Shawn moved to sit in front. She held up a hand. "No offense, but if you faint while driving, things might get even worse."

He offered a weak smile but didn't argue. "You know we have to take them with us. If a rescue team reaches us, they can't go searching a couple more acres in a whiteout for them."

"And we can't leave them to freeze." She sighed because she could easily justify leaving them, but Shawn was right. It took a few tries, but she managed to get the vehicle started and drove back to the trailer. Using the hitch, she attached it to the back. After what seemed like hours but was likely only minutes, she sat back in the driver's seat.

She revved the engine, but realistically she couldn't see farther than a few feet ahead.

Shawn wrapped his right arm around her waist for stability. He leaned forward until his scratchy face brushed against her cheek. "Into the prevailing wind. Take it slow. There might be a drilling well that's uncovered, for all we know."

She almost cried at the thought. With the steering wheel pointed directly into the painful wind, she put on the goggles she'd found tied to the console and drove straight into the blizzard. With each bump and hill, she strained to see farther into the blowing snow. They passed a drilling rig and then minutes later another. Her heart rate sped up. Were they just driving in circles until they froze to death?

She sent up a silent cry to the Lord. And then she caught the smallest glimpse of red, which gave her pause. She pressed forward. Yes, definitely red pipe. With lines of snow draped on top of the red, seeping through the grates above, it was the most beautiful fake candy cane she'd ever seen. When she'd made the decision to leave her car, she'd felt safe exploring because she knew the red pipe would lead her back to it. The car, even though it now resided in a mine with a dead man inside, had been parked very close to the control building. She pushed the throttle harder.

Every minute she strained her vision, her arms and her back against the blizzard, she felt the temptation to rest, even just for a second. The moment the building came into sight she almost cried. "We're here, Shawn."

Pressure increased on her back. "Shawn? Are you okay?"

He didn't answer.

FIFTEEN

She would not make it to a safe haven, only to lose him. Jackie maneuvered to get off the ATV, doing her best to keep him from falling into the snow. Instead he fell over on his stomach onto the seat. It took her ten minutes, but she found the industrial-sized generator and cranked it. Lights flickered on within the windows.

Emitting something between a growl and a cry, Shawn lifted his head.

She ran to him and tugged on his right arm until he was able to stand. "I wasn't going to leave you there in the snow," she said. "But if we don't get that bleeding to stop, I fear the next time you pass out, you won't wake back up again. Let's get inside."

"The snow is warmer than the air," he said with a groan. "That's messed up."

"So messed up." She laughed and this time he actually leaned on her for support as they shuffled for the door. The snow, mercifully, wasn't as thick on the paths that had once been shoveled a couple of days ago. "You have keys, right?"

He shook his head. "No." He gestured with his head

to a rock peeking out of the snow. "They can take a door out of my pay. I might be asking for hazard pay after this week."

A sense of humor was a good sign. She propped him up beside a window, grabbed the rock and, with a heave, threw it at the window closest to the latch.

It bounced off.

If she weren't at the end of her rope, it might've been funny. Shawn leaned over and picked it up with his right hand. He stepped in front of the door, and with seemingly the effort of a tap, the rock snapped through the glass and fell through the other side.

Jackie rushed forward, reached her hand in the hole and opened the door from the inside. She looked over her shoulder at Shawn with a smile. "Even when injured, you can't leave me to save the day alone."

"The biggest mistake I ever made was leaving you, Jackie. I'd like to think I've learned from it."

Did he know his words rocked her to the core? He'd basically paraphrased the words she'd longed to hear a decade ago. The objections that'd once come so quickly to mind faded in the background after the kiss they'd shared in the cave. Dizziness washed over her. She hadn't realized she'd held her breath. She blinked rapidly, smiling. They could discuss everything later, after he was healed. Then it would be easier to think logically, to do the wise thing, and say goodbye. "That's... that's nice to hear."

She helped him inside and closed the door. "Let me find the thermostat, and I'll get the place warm."

He pointed to the far corner. "Phone first."

His breathing pattern started to resemble a shallow

pant. Her concern grew. They reached the spot next to the enclosed fire extinguisher, where the phone, with a sign above it reading Emergency Use, had been installed on the wall. He grabbed the phone, leaned against the wall and slid down until he was seated on the ground.

Confident he'd be able to make the call without her, she rushed to find the thermostat and turned on the heat. At least the commercial generator had been installed with the weather in mind, underneath the awning on the northeastern corner of the building, the most protected from the blowing snow.

Shawn argued with the man over the phone. "There has to be some way. A four-wheel drive—" He blew out his breath. "Helicopter? You have my coordinates." He closed his eyes. Pale, and progressively more ashen, his skin color started to frighten her.

She gently took the phone from him. "Your ranger has been shot," she said into the phone. "He needs medical attention immediately. There are also two looters in the trailer outside and another two that got away. If I have to go outside to check on the men in the trailer, that's going to put my life back in danger."

"I understand, ma'am, but it's simply not safe for any of our law enforcement in these conditions. All the roads are closed. There's not enough visibility for our snowmobiles. Even the medevac can't fly. If ice develops on the blades, everyone's at risk. Where was Ranger Burkett shot?"

"Near the heart." Her voice shook, despite her attempts to steady it.

The man on the other end of the line hesitated. "Have you stopped the bleeding?"

"I'm not sure." She bent over and unzipped his coat. His eyes were still closed, his breathing uneven. Blood had soaked through the entire front of his shirt. She recoiled. "No," she whispered. Anything but, and every time he stepped up to help get them to safety in the last two hours, he'd put himself at risk.

"Do whatever you can to stop the bleeding, ma'am. Step on the wound if you have to."

"You have to be kidding me." She looked around the room, desperate for something to trigger an idea, an out-of-the-box solution. "What's the radar say? How long do we have to hold on until you can make it here?"

"I'm afraid I can't say."

She heard the negativity in the man's voice. Shawn didn't have much of a chance. The blizzard could hang on for days. Besides Shawn's safety, she couldn't leave those men out in below-freezing temperatures for much longer without endangering them. "Please hurry," she said and hung up the phone.

"It's okay," Shawn said.

"No, it's not." She took off the makeshift scarf from around her neck and folded it in squares. "Like you said, you're not going to leave me now."

She pulled down the hem of his collar and cringed. Congealed blood was everywhere, but still it ran from a gaping wound. She placed the folded square over it and kept her hand on it, trying to ignore the way the blood from his shirt stuck to the top of her hand. "I'm sorry, but this is going to hurt."

She pressed down and he hollered. "I'm sorry. I'm

so sorry. I have to stop the bleeding. I have to at least slow it down. You've already lost so much."

He gritted his teeth. "It's okay. Man, that hurts." He exhaled and inhaled slowly.

How long could they hold on without medical attention? "Should we talk about something else to get your mind off...?" She didn't want to finish the question.

He nodded and cleared his throat. "Back there, bragging about your dad to criminals. Does that mean you're coming around to the ways of the wild?"

She laughed. "I see. Turn the attention to all my issues. Short answer is no. Long answer is I think you were sort of right."

"Wow. I like the sound of that."

"Not all the way right," she teased. "The ways I'm like my father I question the most, worried that I'm not good enough to be allowed those traits instead of just embracing that I have them in common."

He smiled. "I'm glad to hear it."

"So the next step," she said, "will be accepting the strengths while also being humble enough to learn my limits and being okay with that. Like..." She bit her lip. "Not assuming I know everything about Tasers or breaking down doors. Shawn, I'm so sorry. Pete was right about one thing. I basically shot you." Her eyes filled with hot tears that blurred her vision. "I could've killed you," she whispered.

"But you didn't."

"I know," she said. Though her mind answered *not yet, at least*. She pushed away the horrible thought.

"I can't believe I trusted Pete." His eyelids drooped.

"I'm sure it's going to take a long time to forgive

him." His shoulders sank lower. She needed him to stay awake, to stay with her. She searched for more to say. "I mean, you can choose to forgive him in a flash, but the hurt and the temptation to hold on to the anger— both those things take a long time to get over. Well, you already know. You've had plenty to forgive in life, and it's understandable that—"

"Knowing and doing are two different things," he said, his eyes still closed. "But you were right."

"I was?"

He opened his eyes and sighed. "I didn't realize I was living—well, barely living—the same way I grew up. I've been in self-protection mode so long that once I had the freedom to live differently, I guess I didn't realize I was choosing the same solitary life as an adult that I hated as a kid." He licked his dry lips, his skin paler than before. "Like you said, if I'm a believer, then I should start acting like His love is more than enough for me, right?"

His blood started to seep through the folded scarf despite the pressure on the wound. Her own heart raced and her eyes burned. Did he know he was about to pass away and was trying to prepare her? She pressed harder on his wound and he flinched. *Please stop the bleeding, Lord!*

"Shawn Burkett, if you're telling me this so I can have peace after you die, then…well…you better save your breath until you're better because I'm not ready to give up. And you better not give up, either. Help will come sooner or later. We just need to stick it out."

He smiled. "I'm trying to tell you I finally agree that love is worth the risk."

Their eyes connected. What was he trying to say? Loving in general was worth the risk? Risk…

She felt her eyes widen. "Shawn, I have to make another call." She placed his hand on top of the wound. "I know it's uncomfortable, but you have to press hard while I let go. There's only one man I know who would think it's worth the risk to fly into a storm of this magnitude."

His mouth dropped open and his eyes twinkled with sudden awareness. "What would Wolfe Dutton do?"

She grabbed the phone and dialed. "That's what I hope to find out. Pick up, pick up. Please…"

Even though the pain radiated mostly from his chest and shoulder, every expansion of his ribs seemed to aggravate the tendons attached to that arm. The minutes had ticked by slowly. *Please help us. Hurry.*

Jackie hadn't been willing to move from putting pressure on his wound, especially after talking to her dad. But much longer, and they would have to let the criminals out of the trailer and bring them inside for more adequate shelter, though he hated the risk to Jackie that might bring.

The sound of a rapid-fire jackhammer accompanied by a loud, growing hum vibrated the walls. Two men ran inside, carrying a stretcher. Jackie frowned. "Felix? Cameron?"

They nodded and set down their first-aid kits. Shawn barely registered their movements as they packed his wound with gauze. Wolfe stepped in the door. Jackie ran to him. "Dad! Thank you so much for coming. I've never been so happy to be rescued."

"I have to admit I was surprised to get your call." He pulled her into a hug. "But I'd do anything to rescue you, honey. You never have to question that."

Dressed in gear that looked like black canvas, and in his early fifties, Wolfe still looked like every bit of the hero that Shawn longed to be.

A cameraman came into view behind him.

"Oh, Dad, you didn't…"

Wolfe shrugged. "That's the only way the chopper's liability insurance is covered in a scenario like this. The production company technically owns it." Wolfe turned and looked at the camera. "Let's edit that bit out in post." He grinned. "We've measured the winds at forty miles an hour and the temperature at negative ten. This storm shows no sign of stopping. This winter rescue proves to be our toughest yet."

The cameraman nodded his approval at Wolfe's sound bite and ran back outside. Wolfe glanced at Shawn, and maybe Shawn imagined it, but there still seemed to be a coolness there despite Eddie's assurances that Wolfe knew Shawn wasn't responsible for his son's accident. The men moved Shawn to the stretcher. "Let's get you out of here."

"We can't go yet," Jackie said. "Two men are in the trailer. The looters."

Wolfe nodded. "We brought two rangers with us. They're gathering and arresting them now. We've got to go. The longer we're here, the greater the risk of ice on the rotors."

Wolfe escorted Jackie outside. The medics picked up Shawn on the stretcher and jogged out the door. The intro for the camera wasn't an exaggeration. Shawn stiffened as the wind rushed past him. The medics stayed low, running to the helicopter, the blades still moving, albeit slower. Jackie and Wolfe were opening the back door to the helicopter, where a space without seats was ready to load the stretcher.

Movement past Jackie and Wolfe caught his eye. The two rangers Wolfe mentioned were walking with the gunman and Pete. Not surprisingly, both men had apparently helped each other out of their rope bindings. Except, Pete seemed to be talking a mile a minute, his arms flailing too much to be in handcuffs like the other man. Had he convinced them he was an innocent hostage, the way he'd fooled Shawn? Dread heated his bones. "Jackie," he yelled. "Do they know about Pete?"

Her eyes widened as she and Wolfe spun around to see the rangers. Pete reached for the ranger's holster and, knowing how it worked, set free the man's gun. Pete lifted the gun and pointed it straight at Jackie.

Shawn grabbed his gun, still in his holster, twisted on his side on the stretcher as it was being lifted high to fit in the helicopter, then pressed the trigger. The bullet soared in between Wolfe and Jackie and reached its mark. Pete's shoulder wrenched backward, and he dropped to the ground beside the ranger.

The medics pulled back and set Shawn on the ground rather abruptly, as startled as he was. Jackie held a hand over her heart and dropped to the ground in front of him. "Are you okay?"

Wolfe looked back and forth between Jackie and Pete. "That…that man. He would've killed you if Shawn hadn't—" He turned to Shawn. "Thank you."

Before he could reply, the ranger on the left—one

Shawn barely recognized from an introduction when he was first hired—approached.

"The archaeologist, Pete Wooledge, is the one that hired the looters," Jackie said before the ranger could ask questions. "He wanted us dead."

The ranger straightened. "I'll need statements at the hospital."

"Of course," Shawn muttered. "Can't wait for the paperwork, too." And with that, he finally allowed the darkness that'd threatened to overtake him for hours to sweep him away.

Jackie choked down her tears as her dad wrapped his arm around her shoulders. "Let's get in the chopper, honey. He's in good hands. I only hire the best medics for my crew, you know that."

"It's touch and go, sir," Felix said.

She choked a sob until she realized the camera was pointed at Felix's face. She looked to her dad. "Stunt or not?" she hollered over the ramping-up winds.

He helped her into the chopper. "In his state, I don't think so. Let's go."

She sat up front with her dad and put her headset on to be able to communicate with him, though she had full knowledge that both headsets were linked wirelessly as microphones to the camera, as well. "I can't fly above the storm now that we've gone this low," he said. "The air gets progressively colder as we ascend and, combined with the humidity, that means ice will develop on the rotors, guaranteeing we crash."

"So what's the plan?" She hated how high-pitched

her voice had got. Had she convinced her dad to come to their rescue only to die in a fiery crash?

"The roads are closed, so we use that to our advantage and stay low until we're through the worst." The wind howled again, carrying a sheet of snow that blew against the windshield. "Let's pray my tech works. We'll be flying blind for a little bit with this whiteout."

He moved the cyclic stick in one hand and the collective rotor in the other, and the helicopter lifted. Jackie remained quiet for a moment, knowing her father needed to concentrate. She couldn't see his feet but knew the pedals were also controlling the tail rotor. She never had figured out what all the dials on the control panel meant, even though he'd explained many times. He rolled them slightly to the left, and the taxi lights, meant only for ground use to land, showed him the way to the highway.

She looked over her shoulder to see even the rangers, flanking the looters who were now both handcuffed, looked as shaken as she felt.

"I'm surprised you got them to agree to come."

"Turns out I served with Shawn's boss's brother," her dad said.

"By *served* do you mean rescued?"

Her dad, while boastful in all matters pertaining to his show, never bragged about his time in the service. "Does it matter? They were happy to help."

As he deftly flew the helicopter between pillars of rock and over cliffs, all the while avoiding power lines, her mind raced. The snow began to ease up enough that the lights at the nose of the helicopter began to be of use again. They were going to get past the storm.

She looked over her shoulder to the cameraman, noting he also wore a headset. "Could we stop recording vocals for a bit?"

He gave her a thumbs-up and clicked a button. Her dad glanced at her. "Should I have insisted a medic check you before we left?"

The beating her body had taken over the past few days begged for a pain reliever to stop the aching, but she had survived. She would survive. "I'm sure I'll be fine. Dad, did you know that he wasn't responsible for Eddie's accident? He said Eddie told you what happened."

Wolfe's grin dropped, and he kept his gaze on the path ahead of him. "I know I owe him an apology. But at the same time, I was a little mad that he left. I kept telling myself that if he came back, I would do it in a heartbeat."

"I get that, but, Dad, you told him to leave."

A frown deepened in his forehead. "I know I constantly told you to keep moving, to keep pushing, but when it comes to relationships, I can fool myself into doing nothing, saying nothing." He sighed. "Like with Shawn. Like with you." He nodded resolutely. "I should've made it right a long time ago. And now…" His voice broke a little before he cleared his throat and squinted to see through the glass. "Well, I owe him your life."

"Shawn said you and I were two peas in a pod." She enjoyed seeing her dad smile at that and was a little surprised that he didn't argue. A noise in the back of the helicopter caught her attention—a feat, given the overwhelming volume of the blades whooshing above them. She looked back to see the medics working feverishly over Shawn. What was happening? She turned back. "Did you know there is a bird that when it flies sounds a little like a helicopter?"

He nodded. "The sage-grouse."

"Of course you would know that." She smiled, even though her heart was breaking at the thought Shawn's life was hanging in the balance. "I love you, Dad," she whispered into the headset. A tear escaped as she realized she hoped Shawn heard her, as well. She should've told him earlier and now she might not ever have the chance. As the heat blasted on her legs and feet, the aches and pains came to the forefront and weighed her eyelids down until she couldn't hold them up anymore.

SIXTEEN

Jackie was startled awake by a beeping noise. Were they about to crash? Her eyes flew open to find a doctor over her, pressing buttons on the machine attached to her.

"Good morning," the doctor said.

"Morning?" She gasped. She glanced down to find thick hospital blankets on her. And every finger and toe was warm. Her mother sat at her side, holding her left hand and doing a crossword puzzle draped on her lap with her right hand. "Shawn! Is he—"

"About to go into surgery," her mom said. "They wanted him on fluids to rehydrate him first. He lost a lot of blood but thankfully not enough to warrant a transfusion. You both were severely dehydrated."

"I'm not his doctor, but in general, dehydration increases the chance of all sorts of surgical complications and can stop the anesthesia from working." The doctor took a thin white cylinder and clicked it. "Hopefully, like with you, the IV did the trick."

His bright beam of light studied each of her eyes and examined her face a little too closely. "I'm going with my initial diagnosis. Stage two frostbite, which means with proper care, you should fully recover. If any blisters arise in the next three days, we need you to come in immediately." He straightened. "You've got quite a few bruises, but other than that, I think you can be discharged and have a merry Christmas." He smiled, clicked off his light and left the room.

"Having you here, safe and sound, is the best Christmas present I can ask for, and it's only Christmas Eve." Her mom leaned over and kissed Jackie's head. "But I also have an early present for you." She beamed and handed Jackie a plush royal blue robe with white trim. "I think you have time to see him before they wheel him into surgery."

"You have a visitor," Wolfe said.

Shawn looked up to find Jackie glancing between him and her dad with questions in her eyes.

Wolfe stood. "The bullet must have hit the ground, then ricocheted upward. They think it's closer to his clavicle than his heart." He picked up his jacket. "I think I'm going to check on the other lady we rescued last night."

Jackie's eyes widened. "What other lady?"

"We found a car stuck in the snow on the highway right after you fell asleep. Pulled her out and brought her here with us." Wolfe beamed. "A winter rescue special was a great idea. I think we might make it an annual thing." He held up a finger. "All dramatized, though. Don't get any ideas."

"Never again, if we can help it, Dad."

"Okay, I'm going," Wolfe announced with a chuckle as he left them alone.

Shawn searched for the right thing to say, the right way to say it. "You must have gotten an upgrade on your hospital robe."

"Mom brought me one," she said. "They think I'm getting discharged later today. I'm properly hydrated again." Her smile faltered. "I wanted to make sure I saw you before— I mean, I wanted to tell you…" Her voice shook. "Are you okay?"

"Well, they gave me some localized pain medicine, but I'm sure I'll feel better after surgery."

An orderly with a gurney began to enter the room.

"I'm so sorry," Jackie told him. "Can I have another minute? We'll be quick."

The man hesitated but nodded and stepped back into the hallway to give them privacy.

The time crunch caused Shawn's heart to race, because though he thought he had a good prognosis, the surgeon had explained that gunshot victims always had a risk of complications. "I…uh…know I'm going to make mistakes and sometimes it's going to hurt, but as I've told you, it's worth it."

She tilted her head. "What?"

Her puzzled expression made him smile whether he felt like it or not. "I love you, Jackie. That's what I'm trying to say. I'd rather risk my heart breaking again than not tell you." He watched her closely for a reaction. Her forehead smoothed and her cheeks flushed a rosy pink. Down the hall, bells could be heard, and the soft singing of "Silent Night" started.

She stepped closer. "I heard carolers were allowed

to visit today." She grinned. "I'm going to make mistakes, too, Shawn. A lot. But I love you, too."

He reached for her hand. Her warm fingers wrapped around his. "Since you can't get up, let me help you out." She bent over and brushed a soft kiss over his lips. She straightened. "Get some rest, Shawn. I want tomorrow to be the first of many Christmases with you."

"About that…" His heart pounded. "I know we have a lot to figure out, still, but if we're going to date again, I want to be honest with your brother. I need to ask him for his blessing."

She groaned. "A merry Christmas is in my reach and it all rests on my brother?" She winked. "I guess it's a good thing I have time to shop for his gift today."

He laughed and squeezed her hand as the orderly returned. "I have no intention of giving up, Jackie."

And with the promise of a future on her lips, she kissed him right before they wheeled him away.

Jackie rushed around her parents' house, gathering her purse and her coat. She wanted to visit Shawn at the hospital before enjoying the Christmas meal and presents time with her family.

Eddie and his wife, Sienna, who was now six months pregnant, entered the living room. Sienna placed a plate of gingerbread cookies on the coffee table and pushed Eddie's hand away. "It's not time to eat them yet."

"Will you tell Mom and Dad I'm making a run to the hospital before visiting hours are over?" Jackie asked.

The doorbell rang. Jackie looked at Eddie, who was smiling. "Go on and get it," he said.

She fought against rolling her eyes, stepped into the entryway and opened the door. Mom and Dad stood on either side of— "Shawn!"

She moved to hug his neck and stopped short, seeing the bandaging around his shoulder. He laughed and used his right arm to hug her. "I'm okay."

"Medical staff there are good friends," her dad said.

"Because you've brought them so much business," her mom said dryly. "They threatened to start you a punch card you're such a regular."

"And they let me sneak him out for a Christmas meal," he finished. "As far as anyone knows, he's just taking a walk in the halls for a couple hours. We just need him back by ten."

"Let's not keep them in the cold, honey," her mom said.

Shawn's mouth twitched from trying not to laugh.

"We have a quick errand," Dad said, "and we'll be right back to serve Christmas dinner."

"Everything is in the warmer," her mom added. They turned, arm in arm, and returned to the Range Rover.

Shawn stepped inside and Jackie closed the door behind him. He glanced at her purse and coat. "Going somewhere?"

She removed her coat. "I was on my way to see you. I have news."

"Oh?"

"The FBI caught the two men and recovered all of the antiquities."

His shoulders dropped and he beamed. "Good. That's a load off my mind."

"And my sources say Pete wants a deal, so he's giving them the information on the buyer. The FBI hopes to set up a sting and recover even more artifacts."

Shawn shook his head. "Pete always wanted to be responsible for a big archaeological find. Never imagined it would be from behind bars."

She looked to the floor, overcome by a sudden burst of shyness. "And I wanted to write everything down while it was fresh, so I've been working nonstop ever since I was discharged. I got word yesterday that two of my articles are scheduled to be printed. The article I was assigned about the sabotage will be front page tomorrow, and after your challenge, I decided to go ahead and write a piece on the importance of preserving history and heritage." She couldn't help but grin. "And that story will be in Tuesday's edition."

"Congratulations. I never doubted you."

"My boss wants us to talk about what other ideas I've been holding out on him. So thank you for the push to go for it."

"Hey, guys, the party is in here," Eddie called from the living room.

"Right." Shawn nodded as he inhaled, as if preparing for battle. He made a beeline straight for Eddie, and they did their special handshake that ended in a thumbs-up.

For a split second, it was almost like taking a time machine back to when they were kids, before Shawn really looked at her as anything more than Eddie's sister who tagged along for everything. "Hey, man. I don't have much time before your parents get back, so I need to get straight to the point. I'm here because I know you made me promise not to date Jackie because you were worried about—"

"Nope," her brother said, holding a hand out. "I wasn't worried about anything. That's not why I made you promise."

His wife reentered the living room with two cups brimming with coffee. She handed a mug to Eddie and perched on the armrest of his chair. "Made him promise what?" she asked.

"That he would never date my sister," Eddie said. Sienna exchanged a look with him that Jackie couldn't read.

Eddie reached for her hand as Sienna asked, "And why would you do that?"

Eddie nodded toward Shawn. "Because he dated Miranda even though I'd liked her first—when I knew good and well that he really liked my sister. When he finally got smart enough to break up with Miranda, she still wouldn't go out with me."

"But you're married now," Jackie interjected. Of all the immature reasons…

"Happily," Eddie said with a beaming smile and a nod. "I was young and foolish back then." His wife turned to him and they only had eyes for each other.

"I was young and foolish back then, too," Shawn said.

Eddie shook his head. "Nope," he said, in a teasing voice. "It's the principle of the thing. A promise is a promise." His wife laughed as if in on the joke.

"Even though you lied about the reason for the promise." Jackie rolled her eyes. "That's ridiculous."

Shawn turned to Jackie and reached for her hand.

"See, the thing is, I love Jackie." He looked deeply into her eyes and her legs almost turned to jelly. "I only promised not to date you."

He took a step backward and dropped to one knee.

Eddie and Sienna gasped. "Are you serious?" Eddie asked.

Shawn didn't turn away from Jackie. "Would you—"

"Are you sure?" The question rushed out of her mouth before he could ask anything.

He grinned. "I've never been so sure. Will you do me the honor—"

"Okay, I changed my mind. You can date. Joke's over," Eddie shouted. "Great. Dad's going to kill me when he hears this is my fault."

His wife leaned over, grabbed the plate of gingerbread men and placed them in his lap. "Honey, let's just watch. It's a beautiful moment," Sienna whispered.

Jackie angled away so they weren't in her view.

Shawn took a deep breath and restarted. "Will you do me the honor of being my wife?"

"Yes." She helped him return to standing and kissed him heartily. "I love you, you know?"

"I love you, too."

"So much so that when we get back from our honeymoon, which will be in a proper hotel, I'll happily build a snow cave."

"You'd build a snow cave for me?"

"With you," she clarified with a laugh. "But I'd like to be back to indoor plumbing and central heat by nighttime." The reality of their situation, however much she wanted to shove it back into the recesses of her mind, couldn't be ignored. "We have a lot to fig-ure out, though. The long-distance…"

"I think I have a solution." He grinned. "Your dad offered me a job to start a Boise field office. I'd get to run all the survival courses I want and lay down my badge."

"That's not all," her dad said from the hallway. Jackie spun around, realizing her parents must have returned and pulled into the connecting garage this time around. "I sent my network the preliminary clips from the rescue and they want to have a chat with you about future possibilities."

Shawn's eyes lit up. Jackie realized they were so close together, having just got engaged, and she won-dered how her dad would take it. She'd always imag-ined her future fiancé would've asked her father first. She looked into Shawn's eyes, wondering how he was feeling. Except, instead of any apprehension or em-barrassment, he flashed her dad a thumbs-up before turning back to her. "Your dad actually told me that as far as he was concerned, I was part of the family."

Her mom and dad stepped farther into the room, holding wrapped packages with Shawn's name on them. Their little errand must have been to get him presents, then. "And Shawn told me," her dad added, "that with all due respect, he'd like to join the fam-ily in a different way, as an in-law. Can I assume this little conversation means we have some good news?"

Eddie held up a gingerbread man. "It was all my doing, Dad. Gave them the little push they needed. They're engaged!"

Shawn laughed and wrapped his free arm around

her waist to pull her in closer. He understood their playful sibling rivalry almost better than she did. His lips gently touched hers. "Merry Christmas."

"Merry Christmas," she whispered as she returned his kiss. She was never so happy to be home for Christmas.

* * * * *

If you enjoyed Wilderness Sabotage, *look for these other books by Heather Woodhaven:*

Tracking Secrets
Credible Threat
Protected Secrets

Dear Reader,

Thank you for joining me on the wild Christmas adventure in Idaho. My poor family had to live with me cranking up the heat during an unseasonably warm fall. I could not stop shivering as I wrote about being trapped in the winter conditions. So this Christmas, I'm thankful, more than ever, for shelter and heat.

Love conquers all. The underlying theme appears in every romance I write or read, but Christmas is a personal reminder that I can love because He first loved me. That's the Christmas memory I want to keep close to my heart this season. I hope you do, as well.

Merry Christmas,
Heather Woodhaven

COMING NEXT MONTH FROM
Love Inspired Suspense

Available November 3, 2020

DELAYED JUSTICE
True Blue K-9 Unit: Brooklyn • by Shirlee McCoy

When a man who looks just like her mother's murderer shoots at Sasha Eastman in a diner, detective Bradley McGregor and his K-9 partner, King, rescue her. But can they figure out how someone who's supposed to be dead is stalking Sasha?

COVERT AMISH CHRISTMAS
by Mary Alford

On the run for her life, former CIA agent Victoria Kauffman's determined to find evidence to catch the corrupt agents who killed her partner. But when her Christmas hideout in Amish country is discovered, the sole person she can trust to help her survive is widower Aaron Shetler.

HUNTED FOR CHRISTMAS
by Jill Elizabeth Nelson

A mole has framed undercover DEA agent Rogan McNally, and now his own agency *and* the drug cartel he infiltrated are after him. When he's wounded just as a snowstorm hits, a rural barn's the only nearby shelter. But can he keep the ranch owner, Trina Lopez—and himself—alive through the holidays?

FATAL IDENTITY
by Jodie Bailey

At her partner's Christmas wedding in the mountains, deputy US marshal Dana Santiago's almost abducted. The quick actions of Alex "Rich" Richardson save her, but the kidnapping attempts don't stop. And if Dana wants to live, she and Rich must uncover her family's dark past...

GRAVE CHRISTMAS SECRETS
by Sharee Stover

At a prehistoric site, forensic anthropologist Taya McGill uncovers a recently buried body—and immediately becomes a target. Now undercover ATF agent Keegan Stryker must guard her as they figure out who is willing to kill to make sure this murder stays unsolved.

DANGEROUS DECEPTION
by Evelyn M. Hill

Rachel Garrett has the ideal life: a job in a small town where she's surrounded by people she loves and trusts—until Michael Sullivan arrives and insists everything she thinks she knows is a lie. But can he convince her she's being drugged and brainwashed before it's too late?

LISCNM1020

SPECIAL EXCERPT FROM

LOVE INSPIRED SUSPENSE
INSPIRATIONAL ROMANCE

*A journalist must rely on a K-9 officer when danger
from the past returns to stalk her.*

Read on for a sneak preview of
Delayed Justice *by Shirlee McCoy,*
the next book in the
True Blue K-9 Unit: Brooklyn series,
available November 2020 from Love Inspired Suspense.

Sasha Eastman had never been afraid to stand on a
crowded street corner in Sheepshead Bay, New York.
She knew the ebb of city life—the busy, noisy, thriving
world of people and vehicles and emergency sirens. Since
her father's death two years ago, she found the crowds
comforting. She'd lost her mother at fourteen years old,
lost her ex-husband to another woman after three years
of marriage. She'd lost her father to cancer, and she had
no intention of losing anyone ever again. Being alone
was fine. She had always felt safe and content in the life
she had created.

And then *he'd* appeared.

First, just at the edge of her periphery—a quick
glimpse that had made her blood run cold. The hooked
nose, the hooded eyes, the stature that was just tall enough
to make him stand out in a crowd. She'd told herself she

was overtired, working too hard, thinking too much about the past. Martin Roker had died in a gun battle with the police eighteen years ago, shortly after he had murdered Sasha's mother. He was *not* wandering the streets of New York City. He wasn't stalking her. He wouldn't jump out of her closet in the dead of night.

And yet, she hadn't been able to shake the anxiety that settled in the pit of her stomach.

She had seen him again a day later. Full-on face view of a man who should be dead. He'd been standing across the street from the small studio where she taped her show. She'd walked outside at dusk, ready to return home after a few hours of working on her story. She'd been looking at her phone. When she looked up, he had been across the street.

And now…

Now she was afraid in a way she couldn't remember ever being before. Afraid that she would see him again; worried that delving into past heartaches had unhinged her mind and made her vulnerable to imagining things that couldn't possibly exist.

Like a dead man walking the streets.

Don't miss
Delayed Justice *by Shirlee McCoy,*
*available wherever Love Inspired Suspense books
and ebooks are sold.*

LoveInspired.com

Get 4 FREE REWARDS!

We'll send you 2 FREE Books plus 2 FREE Mystery Gifts.

Love Inspired Suspense books showcase how courage and optimism unite in stories of faith and love in the face of danger.

FREE Value Over $20

YES! Please send me 2 FREE Love Inspired Suspense novels and my 2 FREE mystery gifts (gifts are worth about $10 retail). After receiving them, if I don't wish to receive any more books, I can return the shipping statement marked "cancel." If I don't cancel, I will receive 6 brand-new novels every month and be billed just $5.24 each for the regular-print edition or $5.99 each for the larger-print edition in the U.S., or $5.74 each for the regular-print edition or $6.24 each for the larger-print edition in Canada. That's a savings of at least 13% off the cover price. It's quite a bargain! Shipping and handling is just 50¢ per book in the U.S. and $1.25 per book in Canada.* I understand that accepting the 2 free books and gifts places me under no obligation to buy anything. I can always return a shipment and cancel at any time. The free books and gifts are mine to keep no matter what I decide.

Choose one: ☐ **Love Inspired Suspense Regular-Print** (153/353 IDN GNWN) ☐ **Love Inspired Suspense Larger-Print** (107/307 IDN GNWN)

Name (please print)

Address   Apt. #

City   State/Province   Zip/Postal Code

Email: Please check this box ☐ if you would like to receive newsletters and promotional emails from Harlequin Enterprises ULC and its affiliates. You can unsubscribe anytime.

Mail to the **Reader Service:**
IN U.S.A.: P.O. Box 1341, Buffalo, NY 14240-8531
IN CANADA: P.O. Box 603, Fort Erie, Ontario L2A 5X3

Want to try 2 free books from another series? Call 1-800-873-8635 or visit www.ReaderService.com.